STOLEN GODS

A Novel

ANAND

Translated from the Malayalam by
CHETANA SACHIDANANDAN

THORNBIRD
NIYOGI BOOKS

Published by
NIYOGI BOOKS
Block D, Building No. 77,
Okhla Industrial Area, Phase-I,
New Delhi-110 020, INDIA
Tel: 011-26818960, +91 7428978881
Email: niyogibooks@gmail.com
Website: www.niyogibooksindia.com

Editor: Subhrojyoti Mukherjee
Design: Nadeem Ahmed
Cover design: Amit Malhotra

ISBN: 978-81-992494-2-4
Publication: 2026

Printed at Niyogi Offset Pvt. Ltd., New Delhi, India

To the wilderness lying beyond

the seemingly orderly world before us

ONE

'You cannot win this game.'

'I know.'

Ganeshan looked up at Cawasji. Without taking his eyes off the board, Cawasji added, 'I still want to take it to a conclusion.'

'In case I make a mistake on the way?'

'You won't. Besides…we should keep blunders out of this.'

'Yes, blunders and miracles. The question, then, is how long we can keep the game going.'

Cawasji raised his eyes and shook his head. 'No, the question is whether one should give up and retire or face the choice of winning or losing.'

'You mean even losing is better than leaving it unfinished, inconclusive?'

A smile appeared under Cawasji's reddish mustache, which unusually had not been in evidence today. Ganeshan noticed, as if for the first time, his friend's slightly reddish hair and pale complexion.

'Despair is man's constant companion,' said Cawasji. 'The reasons could be many. In our times, the only choice one has is whether to go the full distance in a matter.'

'What matter?'

Cawasji shrugged. 'Any matter, every. We see movements started with so much passion being abandoned halfway; righteous wars ending with no resolution. Even rivers diverted, not reaching the sea. To really conclude something appears to be a luxury reserved only for small goals, short distances, smaller groups of people. Perhaps a family meeting, a TV programme, a sexual act, or even a chess game, but only if that too doesn't end in a stalemate!'

As Ganeshan turned the word 'stalemate' over in his mind, Cawasji returned to the board, picking up his black knight. The craftsmanship of the piece was such that its eyes and ears stood out sharply but not its bridles and blinders, Ganeshan noted, as Cawasji moved it.

Ganeshan made the final move, trapping Cawasji's king in his square, stood up and stretched. Cawasji, too, left his seat and both picked up their forgotten drinks.

'I didn't really get the concept of stalemate you mentioned at the seminar today,' Ganeshan mused. 'But what I find interesting is the role of "stalemate" in the game of chess. Games like cricket and football end in a draw because overs or time runs out. Factors external to the game. But in chess, "stalemate" is an inbuilt possibility, independent of time. As if an acknowledgement of the futility of our efforts.'

Cawasji laughed.

'This is exactly why games that can be completed become important! Why it is essential to run till the end, even if defeat is a certainty!'

Cawasji escorted Ganeshan to the door. Cold winter air rushed in. Ganeshan buttoned his coat and wound the muffler round his neck as he stepped out. 'I didn't realise it was this late. Please apologise to madam for me,' Cawasji said.

'Oh, Naseema returns late, often much later than me,' Ganeshan replied.

'And your son?'

'Aman?' Ganeshan paused. 'He is no more.'

'Oh, I am really sorry, I didn't know. Time sometimes leaves us behind, far behind.'

Ganeshan raised his hand in farewell as he started the car and turned to a path lit by headlights.

TWO

'Time has left me behind, too,' mused Ganeshan.

It had already been a few months since he retired from his position in the government. Initially, there was some contact with the office; people called to clarify things, or sometimes when they couldn't find a file he had left behind. When the calls stopped, he allowed the connections to quietly die. With Cawasji, it was the opposite; they hardly ever talked at work, their friendship, if you can call it that, was sustained by the infrequent but enjoyable evenings they spent together.

Cawasji was not really a government servant like Ganeshan. He consulted with the department on matters related to architecture and town planning. A renowned architect in his own right and something of a maverick, he didn't always go by the accepted wisdom. His unconventional suggestions and out-of-the-box ideas raised many an eyebrow in the government committees he sat in. Some thought him facetious, but he was always serious about his ideas. A few days ago, when Ganeshan found Cawasji listed as a speaker at a symposium sponsored by a social research organisation, he decided to look up his old friend.

The symposium, on the changing dimensions of civil life and civilisation itself, was well attended. There were philosophers and historians and social scientists. Most had spoken about the fragmentation evident in every aspect of life in modern society. They blamed it on the changing outlook and behaviour of people. Cawasji, however, had argued differently. He pointed at the conflict between the temporary and the permanent in cities, a conflict with no clear victor. A stalemate, in fact. A stalemate, he had cautioned, is a state of being. A state that defines cities, perpetually in conflict between the temporary and the permanent.

When the seminar was over, Cawasji sought out Ganeshan in the crowd, invited him home and rode back with him. In the car, he lamented about the state of the city; ungovernable, in his words. Ganeshan did not engage in that discussion, he'd had enough of worrying about the state of the city when he was part of the administration. In fact, even in the seminar, he had only been paying half attention. He remembered how he used to be so alert and attentive during meetings. Now he just wanted to sit back and enjoy being a spectator. Let his mind wander. But Cawasji's idea of stalemate had captured his attention.

Cawasji's house stood in an affluent part of the town, Ganeshan had never been there. As he drove through the gates, the driveway, lined with trees, gave way to a spacious porch. Ganeshan was struck by the modest size of the house. A tasteful nameplate of polished brass announced: CAWASJI JEHANGIR, ARCHITECT.

The big architectural firm Cawasji and his associates ran had a huge office in the plaza. But there was a small working office in his house, too. They entered through there. An assistant who had been finishing up at the drawing board showed Cawasji his drawing. He made a comment on it and sent him away for the day. Once the assistant left, he pushed a sliding door open, letting light spill into the now-combined office and living room. His housekeeper came in to switch on the living room lights. There was no sign of anyone else. Cawasji was perhaps a bachelor. Ganeshan guessed but didn't ask. Approaching fifty, Cawasji was still as healthy and good looking as Ganeshan remembered. He had an attractive smile. The decoration was minimal, the walls were bare, the furniture limited and plain, both in the office and the living room. The shelves in the office were filled with books, files and instruments, but the living room was empty of books or curios.

Cawasji opened the cabinet on the wall and poured two glasses of whisky. They settled on a sofa. While exchanging pleasantries, as if by mutual agreement, he had taken out a chessboard and a bowl of red wood with the pieces from a drawer, and they set the board. The housekeeper had put on some western classical music somewhere inside; the notes floated through the air. In the first few moves, Cawasji made a good advance, but then he started losing his grip. His moves lost cohesion, and his pieces started getting isolated. It was evident that he was going to lose, yet he played till he could play no more.

Cawasji's observation about things being abandoned halfway, except small personal acts, intrigued Ganeshan. As he drove back, Ganeshan felt perhaps Cawasji was just being his usual provocative self. But his words as they parted had felt genuine, that time sometimes leaves us behind.

Ganeshan had not felt anything when the deteriorating quality of city life had come up during the seminar. The city and its troubles didn't bother him anymore, and he was glad of it. As for Aman, he had consciously pushed thoughts of him to the back of his mind. But now both made their presence known. He watched the headlights of his car reveal the road in front; tall buildings on either side and strips of slums stretching endlessly on the footpath. Potholed roads and disappearing footpaths. Twice they lost Aman on these roads.

THREE

It was an accident that took Aman's life. On an unusually warm day in August.

Aman and his friends had formed a small band, and the boys would often come home to practice together. It was a noisy business, but Ganeshan and Naseema didn't mind the racket. It felt good to have young people at home. That particular day there was no singing, they were only talking. The boys who would sing at the top of their voices were so quiet while talking that you could not even tell they were upstairs. Soon after, they all left with their backpacks and guitars. Ganeshan saw them come down the stairs as he was getting ready to leave for work himself. They waved to him as they filed out.

Naseema was still home, she must have left later. She was volunteering at a women's organisation called Saathi, for half a day, three times a week. The rest of the time she worked as a consultant for a small journal called *Water*. That way, she kept things flexible and retained her freedom. Naseema would be completely immersed in whatever she did. Her training was in history and political science, but her interests had driven her to learn a fair bit of hydrology, environmental sciences and even engineering. Once, when Ganeshan happened to meet the editor of *Water* at a function, he had remarked how he would assign Naseema editing jobs because of her command over a wide range of subjects. Saathi was very different. They provided support and legal aid to women in distress. The men and women who volunteered at Saathi were all employed elsewhere and had worked out a fluid work schedule there. Most of them also invested considerable personal finances to keep the organisation running.

The accident occurred while Aman and his friends were walking by the road. According to the exhaustive investigations that followed the accident, the boys were on the footpath when they were hit by a bus. The driver had lost control. The bus swerved onto the footpath and finally come to a halt after ramming into the wall of the bus stop nearby. Aman was killed instantly. Another boy lost a leg. Others escaped with minor injuries.

One of the boys had called Ganeshan at the office and given him the news. His office, a skyscraper by the city's standards, was known for its architectural beauty. But inside, it was a decrepit admission of the ineffectuality of the giant government machinery. Corridors littered with rubbish, walls stained with paan spittle, toilets broken and reeking of ammonia, broken furniture and creaking fans. Ganeshan had just returned from a site inspection and was sitting quietly in his office, a small island of calm and neatness, when the phone rang. The news had caused him to involuntarily spring up from his chair, glass of water in hand. He put the receiver back and sank back into his chair and drained the glass. He sat there unmoving a few more moments before picking up the phone again to call Naseema. Naseema received the news silently, then dropped the receiver back as if he hadn't spoken at all.

When Ganeshan reached the hospital, Naseema was already there. She had been waiting for him, eyes swollen but silent. Together they entered the mortuary and identified the body. They held each other and stared at Aman. He appeared to be sleeping. The body was badly mangled but somehow the face had been spared.

They took the body straight to the electric crematorium. There didn't seem any point in taking him home. A friend drove them; Naseema sat in the front and Ganeshan with Aman at the back. The friend drove them home once the formalities were done. It was dark by the time they got home, drenched in sweat. The neighbours were waiting in the veranda. Naseema went straight to her room and lay down.

Ganeshan decided to take a bath. Someone offered him a glass of lime juice when he came out. People were sitting around talking in muted tones. Eventually, they must have left. He, too, must have dozed off. In the morning, when he awoke, the door was ajar, and he could see the newspaper lying on the veranda through the gap.

FOUR

Two months after Aman's death, Ganeshan left his job. There was no particular reason to cite. The accident had occurred on a Thursday. Monday onwards he was back in office. The job was, in fact, a great succour to him. The unending problems and tension at work did not leave him any time to think. He often thought that it was his work that had helped him carry on through those six years between the disappearance of the 14-year-old Aman and his return. But this time he wanted to leave the job. He was certainly aware of the void it would create. Perhaps he was just too weary. Even if recurrence of tragedies was not of one's own making, it would be foolish to repeat the same remedies. Besides, he was not sure it would work this time. He had no idea what was going to be his new remedy. He was tired of the practice of thinking, planning and executing, which he had followed throughout his life. In any case, once he decided, he didn't wait. He just put in his papers.

Naseema, however, didn't give up her work at Saathi. She held on to her routine. She didn't show any particular enthusiasm perhaps. To keep going was her way, at least for a time. Something else would cause her to leave the organisation later. Ganeshan did not try to find out what it was. Like the other changes in her.

Ganeshan was not even sure Naseema had left Saathi. He assumed it since she'd stopped mentioning it in their conversations. But she went out almost every day, and it was usually late when she returned. The work in the journal was usually not so demanding that it required her presence in office every day and for that long.

They never interfered in each other's affairs. If one talked about oneself, the other welcomed it and listened attentively, that was all. Sometimes, Naseema took the car out and Ganeshan the scooter. Sometimes, it was the other way round. If they didn't see each other when leaving, they would leave a note on the coffee table with a number to contact for emergencies. Even if the place was mentioned, the other might not read it, leaving it for when the need arose.

The coffee table in the drawing room was a small square, slightly taller than the dining table, with two chairs on either side. There would be hot water in a flask, coffee powder, tea bags and sugar in small pots, a few spoons on a plate, paper cups, a slip pad and a pen. It was a place to sit and savour the brew, either together or alone, as the case maybe.

The notes would be kept below the plate. They exchanged whatever they wanted to convey to each other through those notes. Telephone messages, if any, urgent tasks to be done… things like that. Everything was done neatly and tidily. They had trained themselves to tag their tastes and interests to the necessities and requirements of life, as a habit. Almost subconcicously, especially in those months.

FIVE

Naseema had left a note under the plate. She might be late to return, it said. A contact number was there and also a message from Renu, their neighbour, who had queries about filing her house tax.

Ganeshan was about to fold it and put it back when something caught his eye. Not the contents; the initials at the bottom. Something seemed wrong with it. Instead of Naseema, she had signed Seema. Bemused, he folded it and pushed it below the plate. He sat and pondered. He poured some water into a cup, but it was not hot enough for a coffee. He sipped the lukewarm water. Then he got up, changed, washed up and returned to the table. He examined the letters he had brought in from the letterbox. Some magazines. One was the latest issue of *Water*. He opened the packing of all but had no mind to open the pages.

Moving to the sofa, he switched on the TV to a newschannel. The newsreader was quoting a foreign agency, which contended that there was possibility of a military coup in the neighbouring country. Then they moved on to a panel discussion on that item. Panellists dwelt at length on the pressures the country's civilian government was facing from various power centres, political parties, religious organisations and of course, the army. Military generals had been for some time openly airing their displeasure of the government which, in their view, was not taking them into confidence while taking policy decisions. The country had a history of several installments of military rules but after two consecutive terms by civilian governments, it had appeared that democracy was gaining traction. One panellist opined that the return of dictatorship there would only mean trouble for us, big serious trouble. 'We are already bearing the brunt of a two decades-long civil war in our other neighbouring country,' he said.

Ganeshan carried the old newspapers to the heap of junk in the next room. There was no cutting worth taking from them. His collection of paper cuttings mainly consisted of pictures. He took out one such photograph he had collected last week. Looking at it he wondered if his mind had a propensity towards the macabre; scenes that create revulsion or disgust in others. Did his eyes search out things others wanted to avoid? The photograph was from the civil war-inflicted neighbour. A fanatic religious group had gained control of most of that country. The picture showed two men hanging from a tree and policemen in the act of kicking the stools from under their feet. The men were being hanged for blasphemy, the legend said below.

Ganeshan had just entered the kitchen, set on making some soup, when he heard the click of the key in the door lock. Naseema came in. There was an air of serenity on her face though she looked physically tired.

She brought meat curry from a shop. She placed it on the dining table. As she washed her face, and came back, Ganeshan arranged the curry and bread on the table and laid out plates. They were ready for supper.

Ganeshan asked jokingly, 'When did you change your name, Naseema?'

Naseema looked at him curiously.

'I noticed it only today,' he said, pointing his eyes towards the coffee table. 'But I am now wondering if you have been signing thus before also.'

'Aren't changes good?' she asked with a glint of mischief in her eyes.

'Changes…of course, they are good. But such basic changes—'

'What is so basic about a name?'

'Well, nothing if one has to think about it, I guess.'

After a few moments of silence, Naseema looked up from her plate and added, 'You don't seem to be convinced.'

'I thought the old name was somehow better.'

'It doesn't mean much, it is not as if I have converted. Neither of us care much for religion anyway.'

'Actually, it is a kind of a change in beliefs.'

Ganeshan looked up and said contemplatively, 'Okay, I have nothing against that. But in the new name, there is an idea of limits.'

'Yes, that is exactly what I meant. Human beings have limits, for their worlds, abilities, hopes, etc. I meant a conversion to such a belief, a state of mind...'

'Maybe, Na—Seema, perhaps you are right.'

They left it at that.

After supper, they retired to their respective rooms. But Naseema's change of name still bothered him a little. At first, he'd thought it was one of her jokes. But she meant it seriously enough. This conversion from a lack of belief to one of faith and belief. From the possibilities beyond limits to limits of possibilities. He reached for the novel he had been reading, but soon abandoned any attempt at reading. He sat back and mulled over the possible coup and the continuing civil wars in the neighbourhood.

No sooner does one group establish control, another group borne out of the first group starts fighting it. The new one would invariably be more fundamentalist than the previous one. Civil wars are like that. Military coups also have a similar nature. The adage 'constant vigilance is the price for freedom' was meant for enemy countries, but it can hold true for the army, too, the entity charged with protecting our freedom!

SIX

It was late when Ganeshan slept the previous night, but he woke up early. He had a habit of leaving the curtains open while going to bed, so he could see the plants in the yard frozen in the cold, waiting expectantly for the sun, as he woke up. As usual, he lay there watching the sun for some time and then got up, put on his warm gown and went to the window.

Usual scenes outside. Nayak, of the opposite house, was getting ready to drop his polio-affected daughter at the bus stop. He had wrapped a shawl over his kurta and pajamas. The girl was slowly moving towards the car, taking support of the walls and the gate. If the woman in the next house wasn't responding to the milkman's call, it wasn't because she wasn't up but because she was busy. Her husband Ahuja, a merchant navy officer, was away. He comes twice a year to stay for a month. Renu Ahuja wanted to talk to him about the house tax, he remembered. Ganeshan was helping her navigate the municipal corporation website. Helicopter engineer Srinivasan must be sleeping, but his house was not. One could hear the *suprabhatam* from their place. His elderly parents had already finished their morning bath and were on their way to the temple. The man greeting them was Colonel Desouza. His wife is the principal of a public school up in the hills and hence he lived alone. The Desouzas had lost both of their children. His morning walk, and greeting every neighbour, was a must for the colonel.

Ganeshan's friends from his office circle had faded away after he quit, mainly because he had not cared to cultivate the friendships. He realised that he'd started getting to know the people in the neighbourhood only now. He also realised that some friends of Naseema who had become family friends over the years were closer to him than his office friends, maybe because they didn't talk shop. Naseema had more friends than Ganeshan. That too from varying fields. She was more social than him, no doubt. Rishi, a social anthropologist working in a research establishment, was of special interest to him as his field opened new vistas for him.

Naseema, too, had gotten up early. She was in the garden—a patch of roughly one hundred square feet—she had reared in the backyard, working like an early bird. She slept in the room facing the garden. And Ganeshan in the room facing the front yard. Aman's room—it still remained his—was upstairs which had windows in all directions.

The radio in Naseema's room was playing a bhajan: '*Mujhi mein chhup kar mujhi se door, yeh kaisa dastoor re malik, yeh kaisa dastoor*.'

After the morning tea, Ganeshan, too, went to his garden. If the backyard garden was Naseema's responsibility, the front one was his. A small rectangular lawn with beds of flowering plants bordering it—that was it. It lay between the gate and the window of his room. It was perhaps double the size of the back garden.

After they lost Aman, one day Naseema just started working in the backyard, which was lying neglected. The rains had set in by then. She brought a small pickaxe and a shovel from somewhere, turned all the soil and levelled it. She removed all the grass and ordered some fresh soil, manure and saplings. She herself did all the planting, watering and rearing. Every day, she would spend an hour there whether there was anything to do or not. Ganeshan was not as zealous as her though he had been attending to the front yard from the very beginning.

Once a mali had come and planted saplings of phlox, calendula and antirrhinum. But neglect was writ large. Weeds in the beds and the grass had grown tall. With a sudden resolution, Ganeshan collected the tools and went in. He was cutting the grass when three boys showed up. Friends of Aman. One had on a jacket and a cap and had a guitar with him, in a case. The other two were in pullovers. They wished him a good morning, all of them together, as they entered the gate.

Ganeshan dropped the grass-cutter and stood up. He greeted them with a smile but sensed their discomfort, perhaps not sure of the propriety of it.

'Come, boys,' Ganeshan welcomed them.

'Uncle, we—' the boy in the jacket started and stopped.

'We came to give this back,' he continued, handing over the guitar. 'It belonged to Aman.'

All three were familiar to Ganeshan. They used to be frequent visitors, but Ganeshan didn't know their names. Both Ganeshan and Naseema had tried to give Aman space when he had returned. Trying not to do anything that would make him leave again, although there was no evidence to suggest they were the reason he left in the first place. He also never gave an impression that their interest would be unwelcome, and yet…

Ganeshan felt he was more familiar with the boy holding the guitar. He was one of the boys he'd seen along with Aman at the dhaba near the bus terminal. Or perhaps all of them had been there. Ganeshan believed that, like Aman, they also had not noticed him there.

Ganeshan suddenly realised that the boys were waiting for a reply. Then, he said a bit awkwardly, 'Ah, yes, Aman's.'

He walked into the living room, followed by the boys. They caught a quick glance of the stairs leading up to Aman's room and then placed the instrument on the table.

'We should have returned it sooner. Forgive us,' one of them said.

'Since we are going away now—'

'Where to?'

Ganeshan couldn't hide the anxiety in his words.

All three shrugged their shoulders.

'In different ways.'

'Oh!'

Ganeshan went inside to call Naseema. She was in the bath.

'We will take leave, uncle,' they again said in unison.

'Aman's mother—'

'Please give her our regards, uncle.'

They had no intention of lingering, it seemed. Ganeshan had wanted to ask them something. But in the joy and suddeness of seeing them, he forgot about it.

Aman had a number of friends before he had disappeared also. They, too, used to come home with him. It was not possible to say if these were the same boys. A big gap of six years separated the two groups. Like Aman, they, too, must have undergone a lot of changes, physically and otherwise. The age was such. What was it that he wanted to ask them?

Why did Aman have to leave them, and to where? Did they know where Aman had been when he'd disappeared? What were their names, where did they live, where were they headed?

'Okay,' Ganeshan bid them goodbye without asking anything. As they crossed the gate, he patted them softly on the back.

'Okay, uncle,' they said and walked away.

The first thing Naseema noticed when she came out of the bath was the guitar case on the table. She walked straight to it and touched it as if to find out what it felt like.

'Aman's?' she asked.

'The boys brought it,' answered Ganeshan.

Ganeshan, too, touched it. They opened it but didn't take it out. After looking at the guitar for some time, they closed it.

'I'll take it to his room,' Ganeshan said.

Naseema agreed.

SEVEN

Aman was fourteen when he went missing. For a month or two before that, he had become irregular at returning home. He would be out with friends after school hours, usually playing basketball. That was his craze. He would return home exhausted and drenched in sweat. Then started the long phone calls. You could hear him singing loudly in his room upstairs. He would be late coming down for supper. Often, he would eat alone after they had retired. He started getting up late in the morning. They somehow did not notice the gradual distancing.

One late evening, a friend of his rang to say that Aman's bike was in the empty parking lot of the gym. The gym had closed for the day, and there was no sign of him. The watchman had seen him going in early in the evening but had no idea when he left. The boys usually left in groups, and it was quite dark by the time the gym closed.

The gym was not very large. It was a busy place—an accident or mishap could not go unnoticed. Yet Aman disappeared.

It was May. Throughout the sweltering night, they searched for him, the parents, friends and policemen. In the swimming pool, grounds, every nook and corner. The search continued even after that. Gradually, it turned into waiting.

Aman did not return. That day, the next or the next…so began the six years without Aman.

EIGHT

In the beginning of those six years, the idea of Aman's death did not occur to them. They pictured him in some tragic or unhappy situation, which kept haunting them. Slowly, that vanished, and death became a possibility. There was no particular moment or day when it happened. But even without realising it, they learnt to live with it.

Death, too, took different forms. Murder, suicide, accident. The scripts for each appeared in their skies, and they let them pass by like shooting stars, never allowing them to land on earth.

On earth, both of them desperately grappled with life. Helplessly, obstinately and with a sense of vengeance. They did that by completely immersing themselves in their work. That's when Naseema joined Saathi. Her health was not the best in those days and while Ganeshan was anxious about it, he didn't want to discourage her. Once she was in it, as he had hoped, things started changing. She dedicated her heart and mind to it. She gave it all the spare hours she had after her work at the *Water* office. She said that every case that came there, even though they were categorised as abandonment or harassment or abuse, was distinct and had its own context and complexities. Every case she undertook she considered as her own and dived deep into it with all her heart.

That was also the time when Ganeshan's job became increasingly stressful. Unrest and turmoil were becoming routine and widespread in the city. These were, of course, law-and-order matters, and that was the argument the city administrators often used for washing their hands off it. Ganeshan just could not do that. Encroachments and their removal, sectarian clashes, fires and even bomb explosions touched him like personal tragedies. He could not write them off as problems without solutions. He qualified them as problems to be solved. The exponential increase of the homeless, and a rootless, floating population, was at the root of the problem in his opinion. When there were large numbers of people without the basic necessities of life like shelter, food and water, especially when most of them had been forcibly uprooted from their hearths and homes, crime and violence would be the natural consequence. Once Naseema pointed out that Ganeshan, in his subconscious mind, was linking even Aman's disappearance to these circumstances. Upon reflection, he felt like agreeing with her observation, although he didn't say so.

Ganeshan by no means wanted to be described as a blind and unscrupulous officer. And he certainly was not. Yet, he would tell Naseema: 'We must admit the fact that ours was a soft state. Why should our country bear the burden of the sins of all other nations? Why should the consequences of the injustices of other countries, even other provinces of our own country, find their way into this city? A solution has to be found for these migrations.'

Naseema was not in the habit of speaking in abstraction, beyond concrete realities and experiences within her ambit. She only recounted a recent incident in the city where a Tibetan refugee stood in the middle of a main thoroughfare and immolated himself. The passers-by noticed it only when the flames shot up. The whole event was inadvertently caught by a TV crew who were interviewing people about something unrelated. A young man taking position on the divider of the road, taking a bottle of kerosene out of his bag, pouring it on his body and torching himself with a lighter as pedestrians stood in shock—all caught on camera. When the flames started rising, the camera certainly turned to focus on the action: a human being going up in flames and turning to ashes, pedestrians scattering, motor cars almost colliding with each other on the busy street. What was interesting was that the person up in flames didn't make any attempt to turn it into a spectacle. He left no note, he blamed no one. We don't know what he was protesting against or what he was demanding. Even his identity as a Tibetan refugee was established only because he was captured on camera before he turned to ashes. 'Silently, alone, standing in the middle of the crowd, he burnt himself down. Burning down the burden of sins he or his people carried, and you are here complaining about bearing the burden of other people's sin,' she admonished Ganeshan.

They had grown closer in those days, and more intimate. Even more than in the early years of their marriage. They clung to each other, mentally and physically.

Carefully, in unspoken agreement, they guided their minds so that they didn't step into areas they didn't want to enter. Of course, at first, they had only one subject—Aman—to talk about. It felt wrong to talk about anything else. Later, it became a subject to be avoided. They worked on leaving him out; they started talking about other things; it could be anything else under the sun.

They read a lot, and they discussed what they read. They read novels and along with serious stuff, re-read classics. They were never big on religion, but that didn't mean they didn't read religious books. They found the imagery, symbolism and poetry in them fascinating. They agreed that religion and God actually belonged in the realm of poetry rather than of reality or philosophy. And yet, curiously enough, they rode the boats of myth on to the shores of reason at times.

***

Ganeshan's attention snagged on the first lines of the Bible, where God said, let there be light, and there was light.

'Was it the sound of the word *light* that set forth the process?' Ganeshan mused to Naseema.

Realising that argument for argument's sake was the goal, Naseema jumped in, 'But before that event, a thing called light had not existed in the world. So there could not have been a word to describe light in language!'

'How right! Not just the word, even the idea of light must have been absent!'

'That's because to have an idea you need human beings. But there were no humans, only God.'

'Can one command a non-existing thing to come into existence like that? One has to imagine it in the mind at first, even if it is God!'

Naseema digested that. Then, as if in a soliloquy, she said, 'To be able to imagine something that does not even exist is not an easy task…'

Another time, it was Naseema who picked up the thread. She was reading Vivekananda. She read out a few lines.

'See what this swami says, "Vedanta recognises no sin; it only recognises error. And the greatest error is to say that you are weak, that you are a sinner, a miserable creature, and that you have no power and you cannot do this and that."'

'That is a statement transcending religions,' said Ganeshan. 'Spoken on behalf of all humans. It sounds like his personal opinion. Rather...' Ganeshan seemed to hesitate.

'Go on.'

'Isn't the difference between weakness and strength just one of degree? At some stage of life, we must all realise that the difference between the opposites, right and wrong, strength and weakness, good and evil, life and death is all a matter of degrees. '

Naseema stared at him unblinkingly. He thought that her eyes were welling up. He got up and pulled her to his chest.

***

Once Naseema received a birthday card with no name on it. At the bottom right corner, in very small letters, as if written hesitantly, it said, 'Daughter'. Not only her birth date, the sender appeared to know her age, too. 'To mother, on her forty-seventh year of love...' written by hand—that was all. The picture on the card was a landscape by Cézanne. A feeling of forlornness surrounded it as if sending love from afar. Naseema said that there is a forlornness in anonymity. She read the printed text below the painting for Ganeshan:

You built a home for me
Amidst the world's tumult.
You were the light in its glass window,
The fire in its hearth.

Mother lights the child's hopes,
Mother weaves the child's dreams
While her own dreams she lulls to sleep
And her own longings she buries deep.

Still when a big gift is due,
I have no gift for you
Other than this card.

'The copywriter of the card company must have written it with their mother in mind,' Ganeshan said. 'Every individual has an image of their mother. And every mother has one of her children. So no card can really speak for everyone. When a buyer selects the card either the picture is perfect but the words are not relatable or it's the other way around. It is all borrowed images and borrowed words…'

'What are you on about, Ganeshan?' Naseema was visibly annoyed. 'This girl, whoever she is, has sent it with feeling—'

'I am sorry, Naseema. It might have been sent to the wrong address. All that I meant was…'

'Not at all, Ganeshan. This girl knows us. I am sure of that.'

'Possibly,' said Ganeshan, taking the card from her and looking at it. 'No, Naseema, you are right. See, even your age is correct…is this girl trying to tell us something through this? Some message, suggestion, advice? This painting attracts me beyond words. It pulls me towards it, Naseema. A valley like this, the hills…I wonder, if we can…'

'Is it so easy for us to leave this place?'

'Look, Naseema, we have enough to manage the rest of our lives—'

'Not that. I meant, what if he comes back…'

***

And just like that, one day, he came back. After almost six long years. It was a bright sunny winter morning. Ganeshan was watering the plants in the garden. Phlox and dianthus had blossomed. Two dahlias were poised to bloom. The gate swung open, and he came in. With one hand on the strap of a backpack, and the other holding a guitar, with a slight stoop. In jeans and a jacket. A boyish beard of two- or three-days' growth. As Ganeshan and Naseema looked enquiringly at the visitor, standing on the steps, the boy said, 'Mama, papa, it's me, Aman.'

'Aman,' uttering a cry of disbelief, Ganeshan took a step back. 'Naseema,' he glanced at her by his side and turned back towards the boy. He was fourteen when he had gone missing. Now, he must be twenty, he calculated in his mind. At this age, children grew very fast and changed, too, sometimes beyond recognition. But was this really Aman? Height, face, voice, expression—all was different. Different from the picture frozen in his mind. He placed a hand on Naseema's shoulder, whether to provide support or for it, he wasn't sure. They stood like that, as if braced against an attack.

A smile of apology appeared on Aman's face. 'Forgive me, papa, mama…may I come in?'

'Aman, are you sure that you are Aman?' asked Ganeshan.

Aman laughed, a little too loudly.

Ganeshan, too, chuckled and then he turned towards Naseema. 'Naseema, look, this is surely our Aman. Of course, he looks different, but no doubt it is him. He has returned to us after five years and eight months. Give him a hug, Naseema.'

This set in motion three and a half years of happiness. They avoided showing it excessively. They didn't want to ask Aman where he had been and what he had been doing. They took extreme care while dealing with him. They didn't want to lose him again. He, too, didn't talk much. At first, he looked a little withdrawn. They hesitated even to ask him what he intended to do, whether to continue his studies where he had left off, or something else. While at home, he would mostly be in his room upstairs. At dinner, he would frequently glance at them and smile. Seeing that, they would withdraw their eyes from him.

Aman was very interested in sports before he left. Now it looked like that interest had vanished. All he cared about now was music, it appeared. He wanted to purchase some musical instruments. Also, a good music system, cassettes and things like that, and he had only to hint at it. Ganeshan immediately opened a bank account in his name and handed over to him the cheque book. He kept depositing money into it every month without enquiring what Aman withdrew.

This distance was certainly unnatural and difficult to live with. Still, they consoled themselves and felt grateful for having him back and not daring to ask for more. The walls came down gradually. He started talking to them without hesitation, kept them intimated of his movements. He cracked a joke or two occasionally which sent them to peals of laughter. He read newspapers and periodicals a lot. His friends began coming and going. However, Ganeshan and Naseema didn't try to open the old book. This was a new book, and they left its writing entirely to him.

NINE

What the foreign agencies had been predicting finally happened. The military took over in the neighbouring country. The local TV channel telecasting a music festival interrupted the programme and flashed the news. Armoured units of the military surrounded the official residence of the prime minister. Nothing definite was known of his fate. The country remained cut off from the world; all their radio and TV centres went off air. According to foreign agencies, the TV centres had also been taken over by the army. The Indian newsreader said nothing more was known and that they were in constant touch with the reporters and agencies. All that they had to show were the visuals released by a foreign agency showing army personnel jumping over the gate of the TV centre and the same appeared on the screen repeatedly.

Ganeshan kept the TV on but there was nothing more for them to show. Naseema had gone to bed early, and he was alone in the living room. Finally, he too switched off the TV and went to bed.

He woke up with the coup on his mind. A kind of uneasiness had taken over him, as if a death has taken place. It was certain that the consequences of this tragedy would soon start appearing at all levels including the life of this city. Newspapers arrived late. Being a midnight event, they had nothing more to give than what had already become known. However, they had hurriedly recast the front page and now included analyses and commentaries which must have been kept ready as this was an anticipated event.

The Ashaniketan incident, which had been occupying the front pages for a few days now was relegated to the inside pages. Certainly, the military coup was more exigent. Yet, Ganeshan could not allow the tragic incident to vacate the stage. After all, he had spent a good part of his life immersed in the affairs of the city.

He saw that there had been no progress in the matter of Ashaniketan in the last two days. Arrests, suspensions, statements of social workers, assurances of leaders that culprits would be brought to book, nothing. There were of course a few letters from readers. That, too, will wane now. Social analysts commenting on the state of custodial institutions and psychologists studying the recidivist inclinations in children will exhaust their ammunition. The prime minister of the neighbouring country, who was likely to be arrested and executed and the general who was going to give the orders for it would capture the space. At the moment, it is not known who that general is. When he appears from behind the curtain, his pictures would be printed everywhere. In a day or two that face would be engraved indelibly in everyone's minds.

'See the paper. There was a news flash last night,' said Ganeshan, extending the paper to Naseema.

Naseema wrapped herself in a shawl as she came out of the bedroom and took the paper. She read the captions of the news item and put it back with a shrug of the shoulder as if to say what else could be expected in that country.

TEN

Ashaniketan was one of the oldest juvenile homes in the city. A few days back Vijay, a twelve-year-old inmate of the home, died of torture the wardens had awarded him as punishment for attempting to escape the place, which he had made that day before dawn, taking advantage of the darkness. The boy was caught by the watchman as he was about to jump over the wall and handed over to the caretaker. There was a deep drain carrying storm water just outside the wall, like a moat around a fort. It meandered away from the gate in a small section outside. There were also thick barbed wire strands over the wall. Knowing that it was not possible to negotiate the two obstacles together, the barbed wire and the drain, the boy chose that little stretch near the gate to make his escape.

The caretaker in turn handed over the culprit to a monitor. The monitor kicked, boxed, slapped and hit him on the abdomen repeatedly with a stick. He was then made to run from one end of the veranda to the other. Having finished with him, the monitor handed him over to Babloo, a *dada* kept by the home. Babloo himself was an inmate of the home once but was later retained by the keepers as one of their lackeys. Babloo gave Vijay a bath, smeared his body with oil and started hitting him with an oiled stick. Vijay's shrieks woke the other children, but they were too scared to do anything. Babloo then tied Vijay's hands, hung him upside down from a hook in the kitchen and continued the beating. When he was brought down from the hook, he was unconscious. After he came to senses, some other workers there tried to give him some food, but he could not swallow it. Babloo shoved a stick in his mouth and forced the food in, which the boy threw up. By noon, he was dead.

Two days later, some journalists got wind of the incident, and their newspaper brought it to light. If not for that, the incident would surely have not seen the light of day. Vijay's body had already been buried by then, in the yard of the home itself. The death had not been reported, and no death certificate was made. Thanks to newshounds and public outcry, the body was exhumed and post-mortem was carried out. A case was registered, and the police launched an investigation.

Ganeshan was specially caught up by the case because of what he had heard of the institution while he was in service. Long ago, a wealthy philanthropist had started it as an orphanage. Constructing enough sheds in a plot of two acres, the god-fearing Sethji ran it under his personal supervision. After his death his sons neglected it, and it fell on bad days. The buildings deteriorated due to lack of maintenance, and the employees became indifferent. The children were not getting enough food to eat, and there were complaints of abuse. At that stage, the government stepped in. It was converted into a home for juvenile children, and a regular monthly grant was sanctioned. But the government stopped shy of taking responsibility of the employees and instead handed over the administration to an NGO. The government's action didn't bring any relief to the inmates. Complaints of shady activities popped up time and again. Ganeshan's associates said that the managers were arrogant and bold enough to defy government officers. Orphanages and custodial institutions didn't come under the purview of his work. He, however, had to approach the officers concerned when the question of rehabilitating children orphaned by slum fires, riots and bomb explosions arose. They used to tell him that a child delivered to Ashaniketan could not have any *asha*, any hope. The heavy security arrangements around the place, the high walls, barbed wires and moats perhaps hinted at the disrepute it had managed to acquire. Watching visuals of soldiers jumping over the gate to get into a TV station in the neighbouring country, Ganeshan was immediately confronted by the picture his mind had constructed of Vijay clambering the walls of the home.

The TV played the soldier jumping over the gates, and his mind kept playing the scene of Vijay scaling the wall.

Then something strange happened. The murder in Ashaniketan, buried under the debris of the military coup, crawled through the holes and interstices and came knocking on Ganeshan's door! Rootless people were Ganeshan's forte while he was in service. His responsibility was to figure out what to do with them, not how to prevent their situation. This was generally the criticism the NGOs regularly threw at him. But he had no solution for that. It was not possible to overreach the limitations imposed by his official brief. Was it because he was now free of those restrictions that this incident touched him so deeply? Is that why it landed literally in his courtyard?

Folding and placing the newspaper back on the table, Ganeshan took a stroll in his all two-hundred-square-feet garden. Nothing needed his attention here right now. So he moved to Naseema's garden in the backyard. There were rows of the vegetables; tomatoes, cabbage, green chillies, curry leaves, coriander, fenugreek etc. There was also a pomegranate plant she had brought from her parents' house long back. She had now planted a few tulsi shrubs around it. Only the evening sun visited her garden, so mornings were cool there. Naseema stood at the door and watched him inspect her garden.

'That bougainvillea does not appear to be needed there,' Ganeshan commented, pointing at the bougainvillea with white flowers growing wildly over the compound wall. 'Kitchen garden is not the right place for it. Besides it is overgrown too.'

'Doesn't matter, Ganeshan. It has lots of flowers,' she said.

'But see the way it is growing, I will trim it so that it doesn't block the sun.'

'No, no. Let it be there.' There was anxiety in her words, as if he was going to chop it all up immediately. 'It has big thorns. When the mali comes next, I shall get the top portion cut. That will make way for some sun.'

Ganeshan went into his room and folded the *razai*. Smoothed the bed sheet and pulled it tight at the edges. Returned old newspapers and magazines to their place. Washed his face. Took the cup near the bed and put it in the kitchen sink. Then he came and sat down at the coffee table and made a cup of coffee. He switched on the TV to see if there was anything new in the news. There was nothing. The general who took over control of the state had not yet revealed himself. As is customary, he should be addressing the nation soon, but there was no announcement yet. Ganeshan finished his coffee and went to take a bath.

Naseema had finished her breakfast when he was back from the bath. Their routines, which moved in parallel, came together usually at supper only, and occasionally at the coffee table. That may be several times a day if both were home. Black coffee with sugar added for namesake. Pouring hot water from the flask into two cups, and adding coffee and sugar, one would call the other to join them.

Breakfast finished, Ganeshan came to the coffee table and called Naseema. She was still in the garden. She washed her hands, adjusted her gown and came in. That day everyone was waiting for the General. Instead, it was a police inspector who knocked on their door. Ganeshan came to the drawing room with the cup in his hand, muted the TV and invited him in.

ELEVEN

Inspector Tarun Kumar—that was how he introduced himself. At first, Ganeshan thought that he must have come in connection with Aman's accident. Two years had passed, still the law kept reminding them of the departed through their rituals. Ganeshan had no mind to go back to all that, but they had their procedures. The case was still open.

They sat down on the sofa. Naseema brought the inspector a cup of coffee, with milk and joined them, taking a seat on a stool.

'I disturbed you madam, early in the morning,' the officer apologised.

Naseema smiled, shaking her head.

Visuals of the coup were still playing silently on the TV. He looked at it shaking his head, then he made a reference to the other country infested with the virus of religious fundamentalism, which was letting loose untold violence on its people. 'While religious and ethnic identities raise such passion among the people on one hand, we forget how the same become the cause of creating hordes of tent and boat people, forcibly deprived of all their identities and even roots,' he said.

'There is yet another kind who often fail to catch our attention due to lack of media hype,' Ganeshan added. 'I would call them the barrack people, the inmates of our orphanages, *balniketans* and *nariniketans*, whose silent suffering in the darkness of their barracks go unrepresented.'

'Yes, yes,' the officer seemed relieved to have an opening. 'You are referring to the Ashaniketan incident.'

'It was all over the newspapers for a day or two. Now the military coup has erased it completely.'

'Correct,' the inspector agreed with him. 'But we policemen cannot give up, you know.'

'You would allow it a little more life. But eventually you too would bury it, as the exhumed body is returned to the earth after post-mortem.'

'His name was Vijay,' said the officer, not exactly replying to him.

'I know. The newspapers named him. Let me ask you sir, are all those things written in the newspapers correct? Did they do all that to him?'

'Every letter of it. Sir, about that boy—do you know anything about him?'

'I?' Ganeshan was taken aback. 'How can I know anything? What is this about, sir?'

'Nothing much, sir. A routine enquiry, that is all. By any chance, did you have an opportunity to come across this boy, you know, while in service...'

'But it was not my department,' said Ganeshan. 'I have of course heard of Ashaniketan. As part of the administration, who would not have? Tell me, how do I come into this?'

'I don't know, sir. There was a small piece of paper among the belongings of the dead—the killed—boy, with your name and address written on it.'

'Is that so?' Ganeshan glanced at Naseema who seemed as intrigued as him.

'Take a look, sir.' The inspector took out a piece of paper from his bag and showed him. A small rectangular piece of paper, soiled and slightly crumpled. Ganeshan's name and address were written on it in English letters, unsteady but without errors.

'It is his own handwriting, we have verified,' the inspector said. 'The boy had sufficient knowledge of English.'

'You must have done your due diligence, I am sure. But I wonder how reliable the information coming from these institutions would be, given the terror-stricken atmosphere there.'

'Need not be very correct, yes. Besides, these details do not have much significance in the nature of this case. The important thing is that such kind of excesses can be committed on anyone there. That it happened to Vijay is merely incidental. There are no knots to be untied here. It is a case of cruelty, stark cruelty…I came to you to ask if this boy was of any interest to you. Since we found this note, I am also obliged to check with you, though the information may not have much relevance to the investigation. I will send you a photo of the boy through a messenger. In case you recollect having seen him. Now I must take leave.'

'His death could be the result of mindless cruelty. Even if it has little relevance to the police investigation, it would be worthwhile to know what his life was like. Whether he knew me or not, now I feel interested in him, sir. You should definitely send me his photo. And any other information you have, if possible.'

When the officer left, Naseema got up and held Ganeshan's hands. Her eyes were glistening. Perhaps she was thinking that retired Ganeshan was different from working Ganeshan. Or was he who was thinking that?

What Naseema actually said was: 'We don't know what is lying hidden where, Ganeshan. The world is far different from what is apparent. Look, such a straightforward case of cruelty has begun acquiring a halo of mystery around it.'

'Yes, we cannot say what is going to touch us when, and in what way, Naseema,' Ganeshan replied.

He went into his room and started pulling out newspapers of the previous few days, papers that carried reports of the Ashaniketan incident.

TWELVE

We cannot say what is going to touch us when and in what way, Ganeshan repeated in his mind. And what is going to lead us where. The news of a piece of paper with his name and address in Vijay's bag led Ganeshan to Aman's room. He was not sure why he went there. As soon as the police inspector left, Naseema got ready and went out. He didn't talk to her about Vijay after that. He feared it would trigger painful memories in her. But when she left, he went up to Aman's room and just sat there for a while.

Not that he never visited the room. It was his job to clean the room, and he did that twice a week. But he rarely disturbed the things there. He wanted to keep everything as they were the day he left. As for Naseema, she never went up.

Besides the bed and bookshelves, the room had two tables. One was by the side of the bed. The other one was under the rear window. Cassettes and music instruments were strewn on the adjacent table. All orderless and scattered.

Ganeshan had kept the guitar Aman's friends brought on the bed. One thing he changed about the room was the clothes. He had washed the dresses lying on the bed, folded and put them back in the wardrobe. He tidied the bed and changed the sheets periodically.

The table by the window had some books and a few sheets of plain paper on it. One was a collection of pop songs. Another a thick volume of stories by a famous writer. Ganeshan had stacked the papers together and placed a paperweight on them.

Ganeshan opened both windows and pulled the curtains apart. Through the front one, rich sunlight poured in and a picture of the road in front of the house came into view. The rear window, where the table sat, opened to a vacant plot of land at the back of the house. Its owner had not yet constructed a house there. There was some dispute on the ownership, people said. Some thorny shrubs with little yellow and violet flowers were growing there. Though not recognised as garden plants, spring visited them too. A cow was grazing in the plot, and two dogs were searching for something, looking up as if they were staring at the sun.

Ganeshan sat on the chair and opened the drawer of the table. There were a few sheets of paper inside the drawer, too. Separate single sheets. The one on the top had something written on it. He was hesitant, almost afraid of touching them, let alone reading the content. Yet impulsively he took them out.

As he turned them over, he found that there was something or the other written on all of them. Without disturbing the order, he put everything back. Then, looking around as if someone might be watching him and then making up his mind, he pulled out the one on the top. It looked like a poem. Yes, it was a poem, no doubt. As he began to read it, the feeling that he was stealing or doing something wrong dissipated, and he became calm…quiet.

Eternal city.
When the bells of midnight ring high
The gates of the city are opened.
The aliens waiting outside rush in.
The bored and worn-out denizens inside
Sneak out of their abodes.
In the narrow-paved lanes of the city
Noise mates with motion, shadow with light,
Inmates with strangers,
Freely and without hesitation.
Fear stalks behind boldness,
And boldness follows fear.
Doors keep opening and shutting.
Dreams walk out of sleep,
Sleep wanders in search of dreams.
At midnight all ties are cut loose.
Curtains fall and all is bared.

Each one out with stick and sword to loot.
Each loots the chattels of others,
Unmindful of his own possessions
Being looted by others.
When dawn arrives,
They wake up in another's abode,
With another's mate.
Having lost their own.
Holding another's possessions,
having lost his own.
The gates of the city close then.
It is the light of law,
Till darkness descends once again.

Ganeshan read through a few times. He wasn't sure he understood the poem, but it left his mind unsettled. It was written by Aman, signed and dated at the bottom. Ganeshan carefully placed the sheet of paper back where he found it, on top of the pile and closed the drawer.

Then, mechanically, he started dusting the objects in the room. Even after everything was clean, he didn't stop. Once more he went over to the table. Touched the drawer handle, but told himself 'another time' almost out loud. Closing the door behind him, he came back down.

THIRTEEN

A peon from the police station brought a photo of Vijay. It was a photostat of the original photo in the records of Ashaniketan and was not very sharp. The boy in the photo looked around 12, as mentioned in the reports. Perhaps he had not been in the place for long, or the photo was a recent one. In a note that accompanied the photo, the inspector had added one more information: Vijay was from a wandering tribe.

Ganeshan was not sure if his belonging to a nomadic tribe had any relevance at all. But like the police officer's visit brought the Ashaniketan incident, obfuscated by the military coup to the forefront of his mind, this new bit of information rekindled a long-standing interest he had in comparing and contrasting the two migrant populations seen in cities: nomads and economic migrants.

The nomads came silently, without the pain and drama of modern fugitives. For them, movement was not a matter of compulsion, but a practice ordained by traditions. They appeared as tenderers of monkeys, bears or snakes, roadside acrobats, palmists, vendors of herbal medicines or pickpockets. They entered the city, pitched their tents in the outskirts and moved on; they had a rhythm of their own. Ganeshan thought of Rishi, his social anthropologist friend. But before approaching Rishi, he wanted to explore the situation at Ashaniketan a bit more, which he thought had more of a bearing on the appearance of his name on the chit than his nomadic background. The person who came to mind was Cawasji. Of late, the government had been scrutinising its peripheral institutions in terms of the assets and land they held. Cawasji was known for his unconventional approach and in this case, perhaps that was what the government had in mind when it appointed him as the consultant for this new exercise. In any case, Cawasji had unrestricted access and entry to the premises of places like Ashaniketan, and that is why he was on the radar of the land and building mafia of the city, according to rumours. For Ganeshan, breaking down the walls of Ashaniketan in a bid to discover the inmates inside was not a mere symbolic idea.

As he sat and pondered over Vijay's photo and the officer's note, unbeknownst to him, his investigation was already underway. The telephone rang, and it was Cawasji on the line.

'Are you home?' Cawasji asked. 'I am going that way. I have to visit a place nearabouts. I thought it would be useful if you could come with me.'

'Sure, I will be ready,' Ganeshan said.

In an hour, Cawasji was there. The place he wanted to visit was a beggars' home situated a few kilometres from Ganeshan's house, along the highway, just short of a huge automobile factory that had come up there recently. Ganeshan was in some remote way instrumental in setting up the home though he had nothing to do with how it was run. That was perhaps what Cawasji meant when he said he can be useful.

The home was started when the law prohibiting begging and vagrancy came into force in the city. The government appeared to be rethinking that too now. 'Examining with an open mind,' was how Cawasji described it. 'That may mean renovating it, converting it into something else, or even closing down the whole setup,' said Cawasji with a twinkle in his eyes.

'Are such things being contemplated for shelter homes of children and women too?' Ganeshan asked.

'Not impossible,' Cawasji said. 'After all, what is the difference between the shelter homes of children and women and a beggars' home?'

'Hmm, open to debate,' noted Ganeshan. 'But at the moment, something else is disturbing me. Something mysterious connected to Ashaniketan.'

'The kid who was tortured to death?'

'Related to that. Apparently, a piece of paper was found among the belongings of that boy; it has my name and address.'

'Nothing mysterious about it.' Cawasji didn't seem to be surprised. 'Firstly, such incidents are not new in these establishments. This one came out, that is all. There are probably many more bodies lying buried in these places, literally and figuratively. Secondly, since you were in the city administration, the boy perhaps had some appeal to make to you.'

'We would never know what that appeal was now. But Cawasji, I have a feeling that there was something more to it.'

Cawasji was at the wheel. He withdrew his eyes from the road and looked at Ganeshan over his glasses.

'We shall find out,' he said. 'We may in fact find out a lot more if we go there. First stop, the beggars' home, then we will head there.'

In the colonial days, there was a match factory where the automobile factory stood now. A British company, big, by the standards of that time. The bungalows made for their British officers were modified and converted into cottages for the use of guests by the automobile company. The match factory had run for some years even after independence. Then, for some reason, it closed down, and its foreign owners left the country. The automobile company purchased the premises.

Similarly, the beggars' home also had a previous incarnation. The whole area, around five acres or so, elaborately fenced and secured, was a tribal settlement, where the colonial government forcibly interned members of certain tribes that were notified as criminal tribes. The law then provided for restricting their movements, arresting and interning them without time limit. No doubt the then government's aim was to settle people who were essentially itinerant and to absorb them in the mainstream by offering them training in jobs and trades. To carry out this task, the government entrusted the settlements to various Christian missionary organisations. The missionaries however sent them to the match factory as their workforce. In the morning, they were herded together and taken to the factory, hands tied and under police escort. In the evening, they were taken back to the settlement in the same manner. Later, when the Criminal Tribes Act was repealed, the gates of the settlement were opened and the people interned inside for decades were allowed to walk out to freedom. The place remained under lock for a long time until it was turned into a beggars' home.

'Here we are complaining about the refugees and nomads swelling the population in our cities,' Ganeshan said. 'Do you know, once upon a time, they were arresting the nomads and bringing them to cities as employees in factories?'

Cawasji nodded. 'That is how time changes,' he said. 'At one time, they were useful; fodder for our civilisation. Today, they are described as floating, marginal or unwanted, they decide whether your days should be peaceful or not. They determine whether you, your women and children going out in the morning should return safe and sound in the evening.'

Ghara was the tribe that was interned in the settlement near the match factory. When they were let out of their incarceration, all the reforms, said to have been affected on them by their missionary masters, fell apart. Fearing that all those people who had nowhere to go would again take to crime, a social service organisation got some land allotted by the government nearby and got them rehabilitated there. The place came to be known as Gharanagar, soon turning into a big slum. Illicit distillation of liquor became the new occupation of the people.

'Look, in front of every house, there is a kit for brewing liquor. It is like the tulsi plant in front of Hindu houses,' Ganeshan pointed to Cawasji as they passed the slums. 'Like a tulsi plant for the whole slum, there is a police station, the Gharanagar police station, which supervises the entire illicit distillation activity. They are the managers or rather the investors of the industry, people say. This place provides all the spirit needed by the city.'

Beggars were certainly not more dangerous than criminals, but for some strange reason, the conversion of the criminal settlement into beggars' home entailed a complete revamping of the security arrangements around it. In addition to the eight strands of barbed wire, a wire-net shield covering the whole fence was erected. A parallel fence of cactus plants had by then grown inside. The only thing the place didn't seem to have was a moat. The mechanism of control structured by the colonial system was basically intact in spite of the three quarters of a century that has passed. In fact, it had been strengthened by the natural growth of a layer of cactus. As for the community being incarcerated inside, it had become weaker, with beggars replacing thieves!

Ganeshan and Cawasji got the gates opened and went inside. What struck them at first sight was that the sheds constructed for Gharas by the British had all now collapsed. The roofs had fallen in or been blown off by wind, and what remained were only walls, or portions of it. There were only trees to give shelter to the beggars from the sun and rain, and there were plenty of them. The beggars lived under the trees with their belongings hung on the branches like primitive men. Picked up from different places, they had formed new bonds and families. The Christian missionaries who were managing the criminal settlement had left long ago. A church they had built had been reduced to a pentagonal front wall, still carrying a lonely cross at the top. Trees and shrubs, fallen sheds and the solitary cross together created an eerie environment.

The beggars were mostly leprous or tubercular. Water supply was through a tanker which came in the morning. There was no electricity. Most of the latrines were, for no known reason, locked up. The rest were choked and stinking. A doctor visited the place twice a month. He never had medicines with him. There was some initiative to provide vocational training and to make them part of the system of production but obviously nothing worked. The inmates were provided with two meals a day—that was all. They were crowding before the counter for food when Ganeshan and Cawasji reached there. Rice, dal and boiled potatoes. The inmates were not ready to talk to them as they were busy getting food. There was anyway not much purpose to talk here.

'What must they do with the dead here?' Ganeshan wondered, a bit awkwardly.

Cawasji looked around. 'Dakhma, you must have heard?' he asked.

Ganeshan nodded. When Parsis die, the cadaver is taken and kept in a large open well called Dakhma and is left there to be consumed by birds of prey. Children's and women's homes were also like Dakhmas where living beings were kept for various kinds of vultures to feed on, he thought to himself. Vultures in human shape.

Cawasji's mind was, however, on accounting. He said, 'Being a beggars' home, nobody likely keeps count.'

They spent quite some time in the place. They strolled between collapsed buildings, trees and shrubs not sure what they were looking for. In the process, they discovered two wells inside. One had water. The other was covered with overgrowth. They also came across a few places that looked like burials. Cawasji did not seem interested in talking to the inmates. Ganeshan wasn't sure why they were there.

The office and rest rooms of the staff and kitchen were in buildings situated outside the enclosure. Standing in the midst of huge trees, also planted by the missionaries, these buildings were a class apart. They were made of strong bricks and were properly maintained and taken care of. There were workers in the kitchen washing and clerks and watchmen playing carom sitting under the trees.

They also went by the Gharanagar police station, which was not far off. There were three policemen on duty. One was sleeping, another basking in the sun and reading the newspaper and a third was walking in the yard. Two of them belonged to the Ghara tribe. They had no scruples in saying that Gharas were engaged in illicit distillation of spirit and that it was being done with the knowledge of the police. They even justified it, stating that if they were stopped from doing it, they would go back to their traditional job of stealing and dacoity. Yet, in order to ensure that the rule of law was being upheld, every month they would apprehend two or three Gharas, register cases, put them in jail and eventually let them off on bail.

With the survey finished, Ganeshan and Cawasji left. On the way, they spoke about the future of the place.

'Our views are but nominal in these matters,' Cawasji said, showing little interest in the matter. 'Time changes and so does society's views. Weren't those the same tribesmen who were feared by people and put behind barbed wires who were let out later? Interning people like this for the crime of being penniless may be judged as abhorrent tomorrow. Deconstruction is as strong a practice as construction now. You have seen the roofs of those sheds blown off. Such structures have ceased to be shelters to anybody. The strength of a structure, let alone its utility, cannot be worked out on the design table. Even if we put those roofs back, they may not stay there long.'

'You are again speaking in riddles…'

'I am not a moulder or even the mould, Ganeshan, just the metal poured into it. Does a bomb explosion or some motor cyclists bursting into a bazaar and emptying the magazines of their guns on an unsuspecting crowd create the same sort of shock it used to in the minds of people? Accepting theft and begging as basic facts of life would be much easier. You heard the policeman talking about preferring small crimes in place of bigger ones.'

Ganeshan didn't reply immediately. His mind had wandered back to the question Cawasji had put to him earlier: In what manner is a beggars' home different from other such homes?

They drove silently by the same route along the highway. The traffic intensified. The types of vehicles on the road also changed. Sometimes, there were more cars; at others times, buses or trucks. The transformation of Gharanagar led his mind to another story, that of Panch Ratan colony. If Gharas were itinerants by birth, the residents of Panch Ratan colony came there as refugees from a place and culture to which they were rooted like trees. A small ethnic group with strong and strange traditions, they found themselves on the wrong side of the line when the country was partitioned on the basis of religion. Unable to face the attack of the majority community there, they had to flee. Honour killing was a ghastly practice among them. When threatened by the possibility of falling into the hands of assailants, their men folk killed their women themselves. Mothers, sisters, wives and daughters of each family lined up before them. With swords they wore as part of their custom, the men would cut off the heads of women one by one. The other alternative for women was to collectively jump into the wells. When the community arrived on this side of the border and were allotted land by the government where the present colony stood, they were virtually womanless. After getting established, they bought women from other communities, sometimes paying a huge price, in order to carry forward their lineage. They formed a big collective in trade and business. Within two generations, they grew into the most prosperous community in the city. Their colony and market were marked with huge houses and posh trading centres. Panch Ratan market became famous for the most modern shops selling textiles, electronic goods and jewellery and luxury restaurants. Every year in August, the whole community would take leave from their business to celebrate the anniversary of their escapade. To remember their other halves who ended up in the wells of a distant village. They didn't mourn them but remembered them with pride. The children of the new generation would present on the stage scenes of beheading or jumping into the well. When they smashed on the floor an earthen pot carried on the head to represent the falling of heads on the ground with every swoop of the sword, or when they jumped into a circle marked with a white rope depicting a well, the girls would struggle to suppress laughter.

Cawasji said it was not possible to fix the blown off roofs back in their place.

FOURTEEN

Ganeshan met Rishi for the first time in an event at the Second Saturday Club, organised every second Saturday. Members of the club were mostly elders, retired and living an idle life. Some of them were from what we call the elite of the society. The programme consisted of an evening meeting in a conference hall, discussion on books read or written by members for some time and then dispersal after tea. It was doubtful if the club had any existence beyond these second Saturdays.

It was Naseema who took Ganeshan there. She happened to be a member of the club, he didn't know how. Perhaps she joined it during the days after Aman's disappearance. She used to read a lot in those days and may have landed there through some author or bookseller. Later on, her reading habit dimished, and she started spending more time at Saathi.

Naseema had warned Ganeshan that a stock observation in the meetings would be that some people start reading after they retire from their jobs and others stop reading after the retirement. Another thing she told him about was the frequent use of the expression 'people like us' by the members. That expression was all too evident in the meeting. In his welcome speech, the secretary mentioned that though the members of the club came from different walks of life, the one point they all agreed upon was that they were all good readers.

It was the practice to invite a writer or two in every meeting, and the guests that day were two 'middle' writers. Rishi was one of them. Rishi was an old acquaintance of Naseema's. That evening passed without Ganeshan learning what 'middles' were. It was much later that he came to know that the term referred to the short piece that appeared in the middle of the editorial page of newspapers, generally meant for light reading.

Rishi became friends with Ganeshan even as the puzzle of 'middle' remained unsolved. Ganeshan used to describe him as a journalist in those days. Every time he called him so, Rishi would correct him and say he was not one. Like the knowledge of 'middles', belated was the discovery that Rishi was actually an anthropologist and a research scholar at a social institute.

Rishi lived in an upper middle-class locality in a one-room studio flat carved out of a bigger bungalow and rented out by the owners. Rishi lived in the company of his books and filled his spare time with social work. A young man, slightly dark and with very lively eyes, Rishi had a little limp in the left leg noticeable only if one was looking for it. Ganeshan used to tell Naseema that his limp added to his personality. Rishi and Naseema had a common friend Seeta, whom Ganeshan had never met. Rishi loved Seeta intensely, but Seeta always kept him guessing.

Nomads lived outside history, according to Rishi. 'They live in the perpetual present,' he said, 'with no concept of past or future, two things we are always obsessed with. We consider the past and future as inevitable reference points for everything, but nomads fail to see the importance of it.'

'I recently read a poem which talked about waking up every morning in a new house,' Ganeshan said. The moment the words came out, he regretted them.

'Ganeshan, you read poems?' Rishi was interested.

'Uhm, sometimes. But tell me about the nomads,' he tried to steer the conversation back.

They were sitting on either side of Rishi's five feet by three working table. The table was covered with books. The computer was on a side table. A revolving chair served both, and Rishi turned it towards him.

'Something troubling you, Ganeshan?' Rishi said. 'Poems energise the mind, don't they? Anyway, back to nomads. I believe that there is a lot of poetry in the songs sung by nomads. When you dive deeper, there is an undercurrent of nostalgia in them.'

'Nostalgia for what, when they have no home or past?'

'Paradoxical, eh? But there is more. You might know that a number of nomads live by fortune-telling. What does fortune mean, when there is no future? We call it imagination.'

'You mean through imagination they transport themselves to shores that are non-existent?'

'But then imagination itself is travelling through non-existent paths. It can be just plain lies. A non-existent bridge taking one to non-existent shores. But then lie and truth are very judgemental terms, aren't they? For example, we usually think that lying is a method to hide or kill truth. If you look at it in another way, we may say that lying keeps truth secretly alive and burning.'

'They have naturalised lie, as their life is one big lie?'

'I would not say that. Yes, you would notice a tendency to lie even in innocuous matters. But there is no malice intended in it. We settled people have idealised truth. They have not. What they say today is not what they would have said yesterday. Rather, what they say today may be a more embellished iteration of what they said yesterday. They subscribe to the philosophy that embellishment or constant revision improves the veracity of a fact; for them nothing is permanent in life. For them, lying is just a way of improving the truth. A revised version is truer and a re-revised one even more so. Lying, therefore, is just a never-ending quest for truth, which is actually never experienced, it is an idealised version of the world. In other words, in their lies the experience of truth becomes wider and more real.'

Cawasji's theories and Rishi's interpretations, like Aman's poetry, were just a sliver beyond Ganeshan's comprehension. And yet, they touched him in a way he was not able to explain.

'Tell me, Rishi, when could have Vijay reached Ashaniketan, after we lost Aman or before that?'

'Vijay was twelve when he was killed. So he must have been ten when Aman died and seven when Aman returned from his sojourn. He was perhaps born when Aman went missing…Ganeshan, why do you always anchor every event to Aman, his disappearance and his return etc.?'

'Oh, I shouldn't do that. Thank you, Rishi, for pointing it out. Sometimes we don't realise our habits. Sometimes there are these defining moments, or events that we have, that kind of marks the beginning of the rest of our lives. Sometimes we have such landmarks for a whole generation. If one thinks about it, it is all foolishness. What is a date after all? A small square on a page of the calendar!'

'Forgive me, Ganeshan, I shouldn't have said that.'

Ganeshan gently patted Rishi's back. 'Let us go out,' he said.

'Yes, I am already late.'

Rishi had to go to the institute. As they walked out, Ganeshan asked about Seeta.

'I must meet her today,' Rishi said. 'It has been a long time...'

FIFTEEN

The city had also become a subject of discussion during dinner at home. One evening, Aman had joined them for dinner. For some reason it was delayed and when called, Aman readily came down to the table.

Ganeshan could not remember how it came about. But he had been talking to Naseema about the way cities were founded in the past, and Aman effortlessly stepped into it.

'In olden days, the practice was to have a guardian deity for every city,' Ganeshan said. 'Usually, cities took shape and grew around the deity's shrine. The inhabitants of the city paid homage to the deity who, in turn, protected the city. As cities grew, the deities and their temples fell to neglect. Sandwiched between rising skyscrapers or drowned in the swelling tide of slums, the shrines lost even a proper approach road. Slowly, they became incidental, and the residents forgot the origin of their city's name.'

'Isn't origins fading into oblivion a sign of growth?' Naseema countered. 'When the goddess of growth calls, the goddess of protection is abandoned. The more we pursue the goddess of development the more distant her shrine appears.'

Aman had stopped eating and was listening intently to them. Then he said, 'But mama, the real identity of a city comes neither from the original devotees who flock around the guardian goddess nor from the growth-possessed ones.'

Both of them looked at Aman with curiosity. He hesitated, and Ganeshan urged him on, 'Go ahead, Aman.'

Shyly, and then with a smile on his face, he continued, 'I do not disagree with what papa said about the forgotten goddess of protection or your idea of the elusive goddess of development. While you were talking about the deities, I was wondering about the devotees, or rather, the residents of the city who might not be devotees at all. Just as the city expands in size, its content, too, alters. There is a regular and relentless influx of people into the city and at no point is there a stable population called 'the city dweller'. Even if you are able to identify one, more than them, it is the migrant or settler who makes the city theirs, who shapes its face. Of course, today's settler may be tomorrow's resident. But settling is an endless process, and the identity of the citizen is a continuously evolving one. As the driving force of that evolution, the city fundamentally belongs to the settler. For example, we—'

Aman paused, perhaps reflecting on something. He looked confused but added, 'For example we, I mean papa, mama and me, are we the real denizens of—'

'Well, your papa and mama came from outside, not you… but that's not the point, right?' Ganeshan said smiling. He then turned to Naseema and said, 'Aman is right. In fact, both of you are right. But the problem for officers like me is somewhat different. You see, the character and dimension of the influx keep changing, consequently altering the character of the settlers. In the past, people used to come to towns in search of a livelihood. Such inflow did create problems of housing and services, but the migrants didn't become a burden to the city. They provided the badly needed human resources for construction, industries and such. They contributed to the city. That kind of qualified them as residents of the city. A significant number of people who migrate to cities these days are uprooted by riots, civil strife or wars in their hometowns. They come to the city seeking refuge, with no other agenda. They carry the sorrows and bitterness of yesterday rather than dreams of tomorrow in their heart. They cannot easily make their new abode their home. They bring and sow seeds of dissatisfaction, strife, hatred and violence, seeds they brought along with their pasts.'

'But papa, the doors of the city cannot be closed to them. A city belongs as much to the immigrants as to anyone else…'

'Yes, and that is the problem, son…'

Ganeshan was actually stating facts. There was no prejudice in his mind, just acceptance and understanding of the circumstances. In fact, what Aman said could have been his own words. For in those difficult days, he thought of flight as Aman's disappearance, and migration as his reappearance. There was certainly no rational explanation for it, but in the back of his mind, he used to indulge in such exercises, perhaps to shake off a sense of guilt that lingered there. At the same time, as an officer of city administration he found himself fighting the problem of influx. The way he dealt with it was to divide the settlers into two categories; those who came fired by dreams of future and those driven by their past. Today, after so much had happened, and now retired, he felt like a spectator sitting back in his chair, without obligations, liabilities or even questions.

Ganeshan was not sure if there were other occasions when Aman had been so expressive. Reflecting over that, he was suddenly pulled by a desire to visit his son's room. Picking up a duster and broom he climbed the stairs.

As soon as he entered, he dropped the broom and duster and went to the table. He opened the drawer and pulled out the papers as one bunch. He took out the poem 'The Eternal City' at the top and put it at the bottom of the pile. If 'The Eternal City' was a poem, what appeared after that was a song. A song apparently composed for their pop band, as the repetitions of lines, gaps in between, row of dots and musical notations indicated. Corrections were plenty. What remained was this:

Open the gates of the city,
Let the city become city.
The city air makes free.
Freedom has no gates.

The city is the shelter
In the days of stolen gods
And hijacked devotees.

The city is the harbour
In the world of open graves
And displaced generations.

The corrections, notations and gaps didn't obstruct Ganeshan's reading. Nor was it so difficult to understand as was the previous one. The platform built by Aman in his mind had perhaps been bolstered by Cawasji and Rishi in the meanwhile. Or, was it that the three of them were pulling the whole edifice down. No, Ganeshan didn't want to attempt an analysis. He was quite happy that he was able to stand with his feet on the ground, without falling.

The date on the sheet encouraged him to look for dates on the other pages. Some had it, neatly on the bottom right corner, but not all. It was anyway clear that the pages were not arranged chronologically. He decided to leave the papers in their existing order, whatever that order was.

Before he left the room, Ganeshan decided on some rules. He would read only one sheet at a time. After reading the topmost one, he would move it to the bottom. He would not disturb the order, and he would not hurry through them.

SIXTEEN

An unusually tall iron gate greeted Ganeshan and Cawasji at the entrance of Ashaniketan. Besides the chowkidar, there was also a police constable at the gate, obviously posted after the incident, who did not seem to be clear about his duty. Entering the particulars of the visitors in the register at the gate, frisking the visitors, was all being done by the chowkidar. Cawasji, having visited the place more than once, was familiar with the staff. Ganeshan too got easy admittance as a colleague of Cawasji.

The sprawling ground in front of the institution was deserted. All have been ordered indoors, perhaps. The manager of the institution was in his chamber arguing heatedly with the caretakers and the kitchen staff. Cawasji and Ganeshan waited for the row to be over.

The chamber was spacious. A big table kept him reasonably away from the visitors, and a row of steel almirahs along the wall kept watch. A dull smell of antiquity filled the room. On the wall behind the manager hung, tilted to one side, a big, framed photo of the founder of the orphanage, worm-eaten and covered with cobwebs. No one had touched it since it was put there, it seemed. The other photo on the wall was that of a past president of the country. Worms had not reached it, though it too could soon claim the privilege. A few quotations from the Gita and the Bible and some common aphorisms were written on the walls of the office room as well as outside. The atmosphere breathed total disinterest and indifference.

It happened to be the visiting day of the doctor, but the doctor was yet to arrive. Sick children waited along the edge of the veranda in a row, some crouching and some managing to stand. Being winter, the table and equipment for the doctor was all laid out on the grounds, in the sun.

Seeing that the issue between the manager and staff would take time to resolve, Cawasji and Ganeshan strolled around the buildings, which Cawasji was there to inspect. Cawasji lit his pipe and took out his diary and pencil. There were five barracks and two other buildings in the compound. Previously the inmates used to sleep inside the buildings. They were shifted to the barracks once these were constructed. Stores, kitchen, dining hall and staff rooms were now housed in the buildings. While Cawasji was busy making sketches and notes, Ganeshan sneaked into the barracks.

Most of the children were inside. Perhaps they were not allowed to go out. None of them opened their mouth. All were scared. Their possessions were limited to a bag given by the home. Vijay's bag must have been removed by the police. No child dared reveal where he used to sleep. Ganeshan didn't press them seeing the fear on their faces. Other than the fear and withdrawal writ large on the faces of the children, there was no sign anywhere of an extremely unusual murder that had taken place in the premises. There were no policemen inside the establishment, the scene of such a gruesome incident. The only one they saw was outside at the gate, perhaps to ensure that there were no more escapes, not to prevent murders inside!

The manager was at last finished with his argument when Ganeshan and Cawasji returned. Cawasji and the manager were engaged in some business talk about the inadequacy of covered space and the growing number of inmates in the place. Then, suddenly, Cawasji switched the conversation to enquire about an inmate called Shankar. He said he wanted to see him. 'Remember, it was I who brought him here?' he said.

The manager certainly didn't remember. He had no knowledge of such a boy. He asked the boy's age. Cawasji said, around fourteen–fifteen. The manager called for the admission register from the clerk and handed it over to Cawasji; he could not be bothered to look himself. He also summoned the caretaker in charge of the boys of that age group.

As they waited for the caretaker, Cawasji turned the pages of the register. He was trying to locate Vijay, not Shankar. While Cawasji flipped through the register, Ganeshan tried to get some, any information of the incident out of the manager. It appeared that the police inquest, exhumation, post-mortem and reburial of the body were all over and the culprits, monitor, caretaker and Babloo were all in the police custody.

At last, the caretaker arrived dragging and hitting a boy. Hearing the commotion Ganeshan stepped out of the office. Apparently, while on his way to the manager's office, the caretaker tried to make enquiries about Shankar from other children. What he looked like and if anyone had seen him that day. No one seemed to know anything, or they were scared to open their mouth. Finally, one boy dared to say that Shankar had not been seen for a few days. He and Shankar were in the same barrack. That was a blow to the caretaker. He started beating the boy, asking him why he didn't report the matter to him. He came into the office dragging and hitting the boy as if he had found the person responsible for Shankar's disappearance. Unable to bear it, Ganeshan got up and pulled the boy to him.

It was becoming clear that people's reticence to speak was not just due to fear of the police investigation. Nobody here seemed to be cognisant of the affairs of the home. Even the caretaker was unable to identify a boy in his charge by name.

It occurred to Ganeshan that possibly many people there were not even aware of the horrible things that had happened in the premises a few days back.

It was finally confirmed that Shankar was missing from the home for at least a week. No one could guess where he could be, whether he escaped, died or was sent away from there for any reason. The manager came out and started shouting at the caretaker. The attendance register, roll call register, mess register and files were all brought to the table one by one. No record could throw any light on the disappearance of the boy.

Cawasji had all this while been sitting in the office room glued to the admission register. At last closing it with a bang, showing his exasperation and handing it back to the clerk, he too came out. The manager was now faced with a different side of Cawasji. He had enough reason to be vexed. 'This boy has been here for three years,' he said raising his voice. 'Yet no one here knows anything about him. There is not even a caretaker who can recognise him by face.'

The manager looked around for someone to transfer the blame onto. He shouted at everyone. The doctor who had arrived by now, more to hide his lateness, added to the cacophony by shouting at the staff for not taking care of a boy suffering from fever. It became a free-for-all.

Before picking up his things for leaving, Cawasji voiced his displeasure towards all and hinted that he was going to register a complaint on the matter. 'I brought this child here,' he said. 'If I knew this is the state of affairs here, I would have taken him to a Christian charitable institution. I would have even adopted him myself.'

'Now yet another boy…,' Ganeshan said the moment he got into the car. 'My God, I can't imagine!'

Cawasji looked at the road ahead and silently drove on.

'Is it possible that no one knows about it? I am sure that Babloo Dada knows,' Ganeshan continued.

'Quite likely. Suppose he has escaped?'

'I wonder how in a set up like this the murder of Vijay even came to light. I don't think it would have even gone on record as a death.'

Cawasji frowned and threw a quick glance towards Ganeshan. 'That itself could be a research project,' he said, 'how it came out.'

Ganeshan laughed.

'I am serious,' Cawasji said. 'It may even turn out to be helpful in our own enquiry.'

Ganeshan looked at him questioningly.

'Everything starts from a name. From naming a thing,' Cawasji continued. 'Naming leads to identification. Identification to classification. That leads to segregation, conflict, violence, disappearance and death. Didn't I mention accounting when we were in the beggars' home? It is the root of everything. So, we have to get to the roots, to those registers, where everything starts. Did you study those lines and columns in the register? Don't they look like the bars of a jail room? From behind those bars, like prisoners, those children stare at us. Didn't you hear them crying, "Save us, please save us"?'

Ganeshan was amazed by the agitation in his voice.

'We went there with a problem of one Vijay,' Ganeshan tried to bring Cawasji back to ground state. 'And now we have Vijay and Shankar…Cawasji, could you collect the particulars of Vijay?'

Cawasji slowed the car and pulled over to the side. He took his diary from the back seat and unfolded three sheets of paper which were folded and kept between its pages and handed them to Ganeshan.

'Oh…my God!' Ganeshan let out a cry.

They were pages from the Admission Register of Ashaniketan. Three full pages. Each page contained details of one boy. One was of Vijay, the other of Shankar and the third of a boy called Gopal. Photograph, date of admission, age, religion, height, weight, complexion, fingerprints, everything. Each page had been torn out with care. Gopal's had come out by mistake, with that of Vijay and Shankar.

'What have you done?' Ganeshan protested with the respect for files ingrained in him as a government officer.

'We have saved three of them, Ganeshan,' Cawasji said nonchalantly. 'Just as a beginning.'

'Cawasji, metaphors don't help reality.'

Cawasji shook his head slowly but with conviction. 'No, Ganeshan, what I said is true to the core. Everything starts with naming. Didn't you notice that many of them exist only in these pages? We have to take the axe to the very roots. And that is what we have done. We have attacked their accounting books. However strong and intimidating the exteriors may look, we have found out that the inside is extremely weak. At the same time, Vijay's story tells us how dangerous the conventional methods of escape are. Methods should therefore be different and unconventional. We are beginning to understand things in their proper perspective, Ganeshan.'

Ganeshan felt uneasy. He suspected that he was on the wrong side of the law now. At the same time, he was not in a mood to retreat. While the tragedy of Vijay remained fully in his mind, the puzzle of Shankar could not be forgotten either, peeping out as it were from the pages Cawasji had handed him.

He was a little afraid of looking at them. All the same he held them tightly in his hand like an extremely precious thing. They were still in his hands when Cawasji left him at the gates of his house and drove away. He didn't return them to Cawasji. Nor did he ask for them.

SEVENTEEN

Ganeshan didn't look at the sheets of paper immediately after reaching home. As if the papers were radiating heat, he kept them on the table and allowed some time to pass for them to cool down. He brought the print of Vijay's photo the Inspector had sent via the peon, too, to the table. He spread out the pages and the photo in two rows of two each. Then he poured out a cup of coffee. The water was lukewarm, but he hardly noticed. There were no messages from Naseema under the saucer. He pushed the whole kit to one side and rearranged the papers in one single row and placed spoons over them.

It was then, to his surprise, he noticed that the photo sent by the inspector was of Shankar, not Vijay, according to the register. His immediate impulse was to telephone him immediately, but he realised the folly of doing that and put back the receiver. Had he done it, he would have risked exposing their private investigations and theft of pages from the register. He also refrained from talking to Cawasji right then. The question, however, remained: how did the officer make such a mistake? It could be a genuine mistake, given the state of affairs at Ashaniketan. But then Shankar, too, was missing. Was it then a mischief by someone to prove a living boy to be dead? Or the other way around, to prove a dead boy to be living? Doubt filled his mind, and he rushed to find the newspaper cuttings on the Ashaniketan incident he had kept. He remembered that it included a photograph of the boy from when the case was first reported. Unfortunately, it was not in his collection as he started making them only after the inspector's visit. To his disappointment, he could not even find the day's newspaper; possibly sold to the *kabadiwallah*.

Ganeshan returned to the photos on the coffee table. He felt that the three children were staring at him from the table. Who among them was killed, who was missing and who still remained at the home? Or were all of them dead? Ganeshan felt that if you looked long enough at any of the portraits, the stillness on their face took hold of your senses, like an air of death engulfing you. Photos of the dead, not of the living, are framed and hung on walls. Ganeshan suddenly remembered that they didn't have a portrait of their son in their house. It both pained and consoled him.

Naseema came home in the evening. After supper, they sat together and watched the news. The General who had usurped power in the neighbouring country had telecast a second message to the nation. How democracy had led the country to corruption and lawlessness and how the armed forces entrusted with the security of the country had to, as it was expected of them, step in to carry out their bounden duty. The General had no greed for power. Once things were set right, he would immediately conduct elections and hand over power to the elected government. During the course of the speech, twice the General tried to put up a relaxed look and smile. He looked awkward, and his moustaches trembled slightly on one side. The reporter of the channel appeared before a landmark monument of the capital city and informed that the General has now secured a complete hold over the country and that there were no signs of any kind of resistance or opposition from the public or political parties. The situation was peaceful everywhere in the country, and the military and their tanks have returned to the barracks. Ganeshan and Naseema sat quietly through the programme. Then they retired to bed. The photos of the children kept Ganeshan up throughout the night. He managed to doze off towards the morning.

Ganeshan had a habit of opening the newspaper first to the city pages. A habit he retained from his service days, when he would first go to pages directly relevant to him. Today he read to his amazement that a portion of one of the barracks of Ashaniketan had collapsed. No one was hurt, but a whole section had given way completely.

He picked up the phone to talk to Cawasji.

Cawasji said calmly, as if it was no news to him, 'If you shake the foundation, the rest will follow suit. That was why we had to start there. Our strategy was right, Ganeshan.'

'Strategy? Ours?' asked Ganeshan, unable to grasp what he implied.

'Those pages are important, Ganeshan,' said Cawasji. 'You should keep them safely.'

Ganeshan didn't know what to say. But he needed to know, 'Has anything happened to any of the children sleeping inside?'

'Absolutely nothing. We are trying to save them, not harm them, remember. We have to get them out in the least harmful way.'

Formidable exteriors and weak insides, the least harmful way—Cawasji's verbal formulations did not seem to be just rhetoric. Ganeshan couldn't however rejoice the way Cawasji did. He shuddered. At the same time, the pages he tore off from the institution's register, which now lay in his hands, were opening a different window of anxiety before him.

EIGHTEEN

As they sat across the coffee table with their cups of coffee, suddenly Naseema asked Ganeshan, 'Something is bothering you. What is it?'

The yellow rectangle of sunlight coming through the door was reaching up to the table from the floor. Ganeshan turned his chair so he could warm his feet in it.

'It would be wrong if I deny it,' Ganeshan said. 'But at the same time, I find it difficult to tell you what it is.'

Ganeshan did want to share the problems before him with Naseema. Both of them had always done that. But now he hesitated to unload on her the curious things he faced. That was what he meant when he said it was difficult for him to tell her. Naseema however understood it differently.

'Some problems are like that, Ganeshan,' she said. 'The more you go after them the more eluding they become. Unwilling to try a different path, sometimes people tie themselves to the narrow alley of reason alone. My guru says that it might not fetch results. Reason certainly provides light, but it flickers sometimes. When one finds the light flickering, one should turn towards their own inner light, he says. Try to understand the self. Peace would find you.'

'Guru? Who is that?'

'You don't know? Guru Tejomayanandji. The swami of Nityanandashram.'

Ganeshan had not heard of such a swami or ashram before. Such matters rarely caught his attention. What surprised him was that Naseema had been visiting such a place. He was not happy to hear it but he didn't say anything. Didn't they have an unspoken agreement that they would not influence the choices of the other?

'Since when are you visiting this guru? Where is this ashram?'

Naseema told him where it was. And that she had been visiting the place for a month or two. Then she added, 'Come with me sometime if you are interested.'

'No,' he said impulsively. 'Yesterday I had gone to Ashaniketan. You remember the place that boy was recently tortured to death, the one who had a piece of paper with my name and address on it in his bag?'

'Ah, yes. Could you find out anything?'

'Nothing.' Ganeshan shook his head.

'Yesterday a fellow had come to the swami's ashram. Pratap Pawan Yadav, apparently known as Pappan.'

'He is an underworld don. Did the swami bless him?'

Dismissing the scornful tone in Ganeshan's voice, Naseema said, 'Swami doesn't indulge in such customary expressions, such as blessings or giving *vibhutis*. Nor would he allow anyone to touch his feet. That is Tejomayanandji for you. But I was trying to tell you something else. What Seeta once told me. The voluntary organisation that runs Ashaniketan is one of the philanthropic outfits of Pappan. He finances it. He is also the owner of the software company where she works, you know.'

Several things flashed through Ganeshan's mind. It was common knowledge that Pappan's activities were centred around land and construction work. He remembered the rumours that Cawasji had rejected an offer to join his firms. The maverick ideas of Cawasji which have now left Ganeshan high and dry in the Ashaniketan affair matched only with his shining integrity. The tangles knitted around him seemed to have wider ramifications.

Ganeshan came out of the house and walked along the lanes of the colony. Colonel Desouza was standing in front of his house, two plots away. It was a Sunday, and he was in a relaxed mood. Desouza provided free service in a special school run by an NGO in the outskirts of the city. After a full term of military service and a series of tragedies in personal life, which left him alone and directionless, Desouza finally decided to become a primary school teacher. It was a school for children orphaned by terrorists as well as police action. The colonel would say that most of them had witnessed their parents and relatives being shot or hacked to death. It was a difficult task to bring such young minds out of the trauma they suffered at such a tender age and train them to face life realistically and positively. Any wrong word or gesture was enough to bring down the whole edifice they so strenuously built up. The colonel said he was exploring an entirely new course of schooling as the teaching there consisted of long and continuous learning.

'Do you have the last few days' newspapers, I need the one from a particular day,' Ganeshan asked Desouza as he approached him. 'I can't find ours.'

'Sure, but it would need some digging. I have become somewhat disorganised. That is one new lesson for a military officer, to be disorganised! Anyway, as a result, things are getting piled up in the house.'

Desouza invited him in. A boy, the son of one of the maid servants of the colony, had been coming to his house for tuitions. He also helped him out with some household stuff. The colonel asked him to make two cups of tea.

Desouza lived alone. He had a son and a daughter. The girl was kidnapped by members of a cult when she was in school. Her body was discovered from a jungle after some days. The police did catch the culprits, and it became evident that she had fallen victim to weird rituals in the hands of an obscure sect who believed that sexual relationship with virgin girls would cure certain kinds of diseases. The colonel's son had chosen the army, following his father's footsteps. He was lost to a war with the neighbouring country. Desouza's wife was the principal at a public school up in the hills and was usually away at the school most of the year. So the colonel lived practically alone. 'Things are not in our control, but we should be in our control' was a stock advice the colonel had for everyone. And Desouza was certainly in his own control.

Once the tea was done, Desouza went inside to look for the newspaper, leaving Ganeshan in the sitting room. The portrait of the colonel's son in uniform looked down at him from the wall. Skirmishes took place almost every day at the borders—these did not rouse patriotic feelings in the public. When soldiers get killed, their families receive a special communication from the commander, and that is the end of it. But the colonel's son, Peter, was killed in a major conflict that lasted more than a month. The enemy forces had, taking advantage of the peak winter when the troops withdrew from the harsh terrain, sneaked onto certain snowbound peaks on this side of the border, constructed bunkers and taken positions. Flushing them out was an uphill task and involved a tough military operation, the casualty rate had crossed seventy five percent. Peter's body was brought in an aircraft with a citation for the unparalleled courage exhibited by him. A brigadier accompanied the coffin. The colonel of a local artillery regiment received it at the airport and brought it home. Wreaths from VIPs, coverings of national flag, cremation with full military honour, television and newspaper coverage—for a few days, the colonel's house gave the impression of a fairground. Then, one day, it became empty. Desouza's wife went back to her school. One of the government representatives fixed the portrait on the wall.

If they had a portrait of Aman, they too would have mounted it on the wall like that, Ganeshan thought. Or, perhaps they would not have.

Desouza came back with the paper Ganeshan wanted. Ganeshan took it hurriedly and opened it out. The Ashaniketan report was on the front page itself and as he had feared, the photo in the paper was of Shankar.

Desouza didn't notice Ganeshan's agitation. He invited him to visit his school, as he usually did. Assuring him that he will come visit soon, that one day he might even join it himself, he got up. Both of them laughed.

The sun was getting warmer as winter slowly withdrew. The days were longer.

NINETEEN

In summer they will ask you:
Where were you in winter?
In winter they will grill you:
What did you do in summer?
They can tell you from your photo
If you are alive or dead.
When the breeze is sharp
And the buds crackle noisily
Know your summons has come.

These lines by Aman, on the next page in the drawer, read more like a song composed for the band than a poem. In any case, it appeared unfinished. As if it was intentionally left unfinished. Wasn't there a trait of unfinishedness in Aman's very nature, he wondered.

Ganeshan's eyes wandered to the photo of Aman's band mounted on the wall of his room. That was the only picture of Aman they had. Aman himself had put it up on the wall. Besides him, there were five in the photo. The three boys who came to return his guitar, and another boy and a girl. Ganeshan had no idea how many people usually made up a band. In fact, he had very little knowledge of music. Anyway, this was not a standard band or perhaps even a band. It was more a group of youngsters who had come together and went around singing songs to the accompaniment of whatever instruments they had with them. That was what he felt when he saw them singing one day. They did not see him, but he saw them. All of them were there, he thought. Or were they? He strained his eyes to make out the faces in the photo but could not tell. It could just be his memory. After all, he was standing pretty far away, he did not want to be noticed.

He didn't know their names. He had not cared. They had all come after Aman died. But it was not an occasion for introductions. He could have of course asked when those boys had come to return Aman's guitar but he didn't.

Aman was the only one dead, among the six in the photo. What was so different about him? Something declared that he was no longer here. Ganeshan stared at the photo for some time. Then he put the papers back in the drawer, switched of the lights and descended the stairs.

He opened an almirah and pulled out an old album of photos. It was quite old, possibly over twenty years. It contained some wedding photos, he could not remember whose. It was Naseema's collection. He turned the pages idly and tried to guess who among them were dead and who living. It was foolish to ask such a question when he did not even recognise the faces. They were just photos to him, nameless persons bereft of an identity, not capable of generating any interest.

He put the album back and took out four photos of the three boys. He again spread them out on the table in two rows. He looked long at them, then switched their position like a card game. He had no idea why he did that. It certainly did not yield any new information. The question remained the same: who was dead, who had escaped and who remained?

There were a number of differences between the children in Aman's troupe and these boys. The three in this collection were between ten and fifteen. The confidence exuded by the kids in Aman's group, and the brightness on their face, was nowhere evident in the ones on the table. If they conveyed anything, it was just fear and emptiness. There was nothing binding them together either. They were hopelessly lonely, each one stuck in its own square. The only thing common between the two groups was that one of them was dead in each group. Those who were not dead were somewhere in this wide world. Some in the security of their homes, others caught within the walls of orphanages or wandering on unknown streets, or just lost in the wilderness of the city. Whom should he look for? He asked himself and immediately felt the meaninglessness of the question. He had no idea how or where to begin.

TWENTY

A photo feature used to appear once a week on the last page of the city supplement of the newspaper. This time it was about two parrots, one caged and the other free. One visited the other in captivity at a particular time every day, it said. There were three pictures. The first one showed the visitor's arrival, the second captured the scene as it balanced itself on the wires of the cage and made overtures to its friend inside and the third showed it giving a parting kiss. The photographer noted that the owner advertised the curious incident and invited others to witness it but did not once think of setting the bird free.

In the main news, Ganeshan read that the military ruler in the neighbouring country had already initiated the trial of the displaced prime minister and had ordered that it should be completed within a month. The charges included treason warranting death sentence. He had, before being deposed, dismissed the General from service and by doing so, it was charged, he put the security of the country in jeopardy. In order to ensure a smooth trial and conviction, the general had amended the constitution of the country, made new laws and even changed the judges. On the home front, the government was contemplating sealing the borders with the neighbour fearing that a civil war may break out there and result in the influx of refugees. There was also the possibility that foreign agents and terrorists could cross over in the guise of refugees and hence the Special Forces had been posted at public places such as railway stations and bus terminals.

The update regarding the Ashaniketan incident was that the manager had been taken into custody and then let off on bail. He would be booked for criminal negligence leading to the collapse of the walls. There was no mention of the disappearance of Shankar, or of the missing pages in the register.

As Ganeshan turned the pages, the middle article on the edit page caught his attention. Rishi had written it. Title: *The Voice*. A young man jumped to death from the twentieth story of a building in broad daylight. The identity of the man was not established but his photo published by the police in the newspaper leads the writer to the mortuary. He was sure that the man was the one who used to play the saxophone in a city restaurant. Strangely, the restaurant manager denied it and as a result, the body was declared unclaimed and cremated by the authorities. The writer, however, had no doubt.

Late in the night, even after the restaurant and bar had become empty, the man would continue to play his instrument, all for himself. Having been attracted by his music, the writer had once gone up to him and asked his name. His answer was 'voice'. When asked, he didn't say why he was trying to hide his identity. When his body remained unidentified after suicide, the writer wondered if perhaps he could only be identified by his voice. When the voice became silent, he stopped existing even for people at the restaurant. Several days later, the writer visited the restaurant again. Someone was playing the saxophone on the floor, just as the old one, late into the night, facing an empty restaurant and bar. It was certainly another person, someone shorter, and with a different face. The writer went up to him and asked his name. The answer was 'voice.'

Ganeshan was enchanted by the story. It was his own experience, the first part of the story, which he had once narrated to Rishi. The man Ganeshan had seen singing late into the night at the restaurant was, however, not playing the saxophone but the guitar. He used to walk between the tables with his guitar as if he was playing to an audience. He would even smile at the imaginary people and make overtures to them. His favourite piece was the famous poem, 'Howl', which he used to sing in his own style. When Ganeshan had asked his name, he had replied in an emotionless tone, 'voice'. Rishi gave the story more flesh and added drama to it.

Ganeshan dialled Rishi's number. The answering machine asked him to contact another number. Then, a female voice answered, 'Saathi.'

'I am sorry. I wanted to talk to Rishi and was advised to try this number.'

'Rishi is here.'

'Rishi,' Ganeshan asked when he came on the line, 'are you a member of Saathi, too?'

Rishi laughed, 'Saathi is Saathi to all. In fact, it is at Saathi that I met Naseema. I am here with a case concerning some tribal women. I saw them being whisked away by the police as pickpockets. It is true that some among them, the Pardis, are known to indulge in thefts. But no theft occurred here. The punishment cannot come before the crime, you know. So I had to interfere. It is always better to have an organisation with you in such cases, so I came to Saathi.'

'Shall I go there?' Ganeshan offered.

'You may come. But the women in question have already left. Back on their endless journey. No one can say where we will meet them again.'

'Leave it then. I rang to tell you that I read your middle.'

'Ah, yes, my story. But your experience. Forgive me for that.'

'On the contrary, I wanted to thank you, I liked it. You took it much further, to all kinds of places. I had seen only one point in it, the loss of identity. But here...'

'Go on, I am listening.'

'The identity question has two sides, I think. When one loses their identity, they become detached; relationships vanish. But it also means that another could be installed in their place, ironically enough.'

'Yes, but you also said I have taken it to a new place. I am curious.'

Ganeshan hesitated, but Rishi pressed.

'Rishi, in one glance, your article draws a picture of continuity, where there are only commas, no full stops. But when you read it carefully, you feel that you actually want to speak about discontinuities. Or about the pauses appearing between continuity. I'd like to call them cracks in continuity or lack of continuity itself. I don't know whether it's just me.'

'No, I agree. But one aspect remains: a qualification of the pauses. Pauses that go unnoticed by us, that we fail to identify even while we know that they are there. One more thing, I would like to call the situation as one of discontinuity itself, as you said, rather than the fashionable word *fragmentation*.'

'Here we go, talking theories like Cawasji,' Ganeshan laughed.

Rishi also chuckled, 'Anyway, some people are sending their compliments from here, Rajani, Elizabeth, Vineeta…'

'Convey my thanks to them. Is Naseema there too?'

'She doesn't come here these days, they say.'

It was a chance encounter that he had with the organisation. Almost a collision, he and his staff on one side and the workers of Saathi on the other. He was in the process of evicting some encroachers from a vacant space underneath a newly constructed flyover. In two days' time about two hundred people had colonised the space and more seemed to be on their way. The Corporation was planning to utilise the space as a sort of shopping arcade and if the encroachers settled there, it would have been difficult to fulfil its commitments to the tenants.

When they reached the site, they were confronted by three or four women. They said they were members of Saathi. He did not know much about the organisation except that it was a women's resources centre frequented by Naseema. He looked about and was relieved that she was not among them. It was, of course, her working hours at the office of the journal.

The women there, too, didn't know that Ganeshan was Naseema's husband. A woman named Vasundhara did the talking. The people who were occupying the shelter were almost all women and children, she said in a way explaining Saathi's interest in the matter. She added that they were all victims of a communal riot in the neighbouring state. Their men were either killed or missing.

When Ganeshan explained his position, Vasundhara said that it was their problem, too, as Saathi had been allotted a couple of rooms in the arcade. 'They have occupied our space, too,' she said, disarming him.

Completed rooms had already been allotted, and some shops had already opened there. Initially, the allottees had aligned against the encroachers, but they, too, softened their attitude listening to the Saathi workers. It was a scorching summer. A dust storm was brewing, adding to the woes of the helpless women and children. Gradually, a way out was found. Other voluntary organisations and government schools that had closed for the summer vacation were approached. Some tents were also pitched to accommodate people till it was possible to send them back to their homes.

It was quite some time after that they came to know each other. Ganeshan's reputation as a heartless government officer had gradually vanished among Saathi workers. The second occasion on which they met each other, they happened to be on the same side. There had been a big fire in one of the slums. Heat rendered everything incendiary in summer, and slums were the most vulnerable. There was also a belief among the public that slum fires were most of the time deliberately created, as they our often followed by government handouts and ex gratia payment. Ganeshan didn't find that logic convincing in that particular case; there were quite a few deaths.

While Ganeshan was supervising the general relief work, Saathi had come there for rehabilitating the children orphaned by the fire. There were four such children. He did not know where those children ended up; they could have been adopted by someone or living in places like Ashaniketan or even out on the streets. There was no system to monitor or follow up on their lives and as a result, good deeds done by many, government officers or others, got lost in predator-infected jungles.

TWENTY-ONE

Theorising was not exactly the problem with Cawasji. His arguments often turned things completely on their head—that was the problem. A new vision, like a newly opened window, may offer an unfamiliar picture. Cawasji also led you into unfamiliar avenues, but as he argued you are left confused if it is philosophy or mischief. Looking back now, Ganeshan thought that his seminar at the Social Research Institute started on grounds similar to the ones Aman built up that day at the dining table. But then he took it to such tangents!

That day they spoke about the goddess at the heart of the city always moving out of reach, as people try to reach out to it. Devotees of the new goddess had not just pushed the ancient city goddess into obscurity but obliterated the very concept of a guardian goddess from the city's mind. Aman spoke of the migrants and interestingly, he included among the migrants not just Ganeshan and Naseema who were of course once migrants but himself who was born and brought up there! Was that brought on by the darkness of the last six years?

Ganeshan felt glad that he was now at home with phrases like Aman's ideas or Aman's philosophy. Cawasji's bombardments and Rishi's research lessons could have had a hand in it. He, however, was sorry that it didn't happen during the three years when Aman was with them.

Cawasji had started his speech by quoting the medieval maxim 'city air makes free'. 'After breaking away from the suzerains of the lords and winning freedom from fealty in the Middle Ages, the towns of Europe came to be run independently and democratically. This made them islands of freedom, individual liberty and peace. Towns became symbols of all that civilized life could desire, materially and spiritually. All the comforts of life; houses, roads, water and energy were available there. Only in towns could one claim the personal liberties guaranteed by the law of the day, for in the countryside law itself didn't exist. If a serf who fled from his lord managed to stay in a town for a year, he became a free man. Thus the medieval maxim had come into existence.'

'The concept of cities as models of civilisation prevails till today,' Cawasji argued. 'Even today, all the material comforts are concentrated in the cities. Only the city provides the mechanism to ensure civil and human rights to the individual as the arms of courts and government do not reach into deep interiors. In spite of all that, there is no peace in cities now. They are centres of strife. Falsehood, deception, exploitation, unrest, instability, violence and bloodshed have all taken hold of the heart of cities. Why is it so?' Cawasji's answer was that civilisation itself was now passing through such a crisis, and it was but natural that cities as models of the prevailing civilisation reflected it.

Cawasji identified the crisis of our civilisation as the conflict between the permanent and the temporary. The old practice of looking for stability and permanence in things and ideas was now giving way to a philosophy of viewing everything from the angle of immediate relevance and current values. 'No one is enchanted by abiding values or enduring ideas in the world now. People are more concerned about the present; the month or day before us. The future rarely captures our imagination, and no politician today talks about an ideology or even agenda that touches tomorrow.'

Cawasji then carried the philosophy of the immediate from political and social arena to culture, art and literature and then finally to areas of construction, town planning and engineering. 'Machines are no longer designed for long life. Nor do they fully live out their life. The technology becomes obsolete before the machines break. Ideas are abandoned before they are fully formulated. When machines, people, even ideas are going obsolete before their time, what can one say about buildings and structures?'

'An engineering structure is designed to withstand a designated load and to carry out a given function for a specific period of time,' continued Cawasji. 'But when we are not sure of the load it may have to bear and have no idea of the functions it may be called upon to carry out tomorrow, then what are we designing for? Why should we design at all?' Then lowering his voice, as if was whispering in the ears of the audience, he said, 'Let us design our structures for the minimum loads and needs. If the load increases, let them fall. Failure is recognised as a partner of our life today. History is being continuously rewritten. Cities are repeatedly being reconstructed, to cater to newer and newer inhabitants. Events are true, but they are nothing more than bricks stacked on top of each other. Ideas are mere figments of imagination that pass us by like sights on a journey.'

Cawasji ended his speech at a point of what sounded like complete absurdity, but his charisma carried it through.

TWENTY-TWO

A cane basket had begun to disintegrate due to long exposure to the elements. Ganeshan saw it lying close to the compound wall as he was hunting for a pot to plant a cactus shoot that the mali had brought. There were two or three empty pots lying under the bougainvillea growing along the wall of the rear compound. When he tried to pull one of them out, he realised that he could not do it without cutting the branches of the plant that held the pots in their embrace. He had once suggested to Naseema that the plant had to be pruned. He decided to do that first. While on the job with a bush-cutting knife, he discovered the basket. The basket contained a number of pebbles, round, shapely and of different colours partly covered by dust and fallen leaves of the bougainvillea. They looked beautiful. He could spread them around the cactus in the pot. As he tried to pull the basket out, he scratched his hands on bougainvillea thorns.

Naseema walked into the garden just at that moment. Suddenly her mood changed, she looked alarmed, angry and upset.

'What are you doing, Ganeshan?' she cried. 'Don't touch it, please. Leave it.'

'But these are very beautiful stones, Naseema. I have got a cactus cutting. These will provide an excellent bed for it. If you have kept it for some purpose, it is okay. But see the basket is half gone.'

'Doesn't matter. Let it fall apart. But just don't disturb it. Promise me you won't touch it.'

'Okay.' He rubbed the mud off his hands and turned back to Naseema. Though he didn't want to argue, he couldn't help asking, 'What is the matter, Naseema? Why is it so important?'

Naseema ignored his questions but turned his hands this way and that and frowned over them as if they were big wounds.

'See what happens when you go digging into obscure places. I hope it does not become septic. You should get an anti-tetanus injection anyway...'

'It's just a few scratches, Naseema.'

'Yes, a scratch is enough...on bad days.'

Naseema went inside. He heard her calling the doctor.

Having abandoned the idea of decorating with the pebbles and cutting the overgrowth of the bougainvillea,

Ganeshan got busy with planting the cactus in the pot he collected. He put the pot in the front garden, washed his hands and came in.

Naseema was getting ready to go out. Today she was in a sari instead of her favourite salwar and kameez. Since she started going to the ashram, her style of dressing herself also appeared to be changing.

'Are you going to the ashram?' He asked casually.

Naseema nodded. 'The swami is giving a discourse on the Jnana Karma Sanyasa Yoga of the Gita. It was interesting to listen to his interpretation of the stanza "*kim karma kim akarmeti*" yesterday.'

Seeing him staring at her with wide eyes, she broke into laughter to which he too joined. She however changed the subject and said, 'You should forgive me, Ganeshan. I became a bit upset.'

'Forget it. I didn't take your basket,' he said gesturing towards the garden.

By then the doctor, who stayed next door, walked in with his kit. Without losing a moment, he got himself busy with a syringe and vial for injection. The tubby fellow did not try to hide the panting that a few feet's walk had caused. He asked with a smile, 'Who is the patient by the way?'

Ganeshan surrendered himself before him. 'Just a few scratches, doctor. Naseema got upset for nothing.'

'Naseema is right, sir. What is the harm in being a bit careful?' Then turning to her, he enquired, 'Madam, what is the programme in the ashram today? Forget what people say, it is a real pleasure to hear the swami deliver sermons. You forget all your worries at least for some time. I have heard it only once. Have you, sir?'

'No.'

'You should, for once. There is no religion business in it, sir. Tell me, what is bad about a thing if it gives peace and happiness to the mind?'

'Nothing whatsoever,' said Ganeshan, pressing a piece of cotton at the site of injection. 'Except there are things that pique my curiosity and push away the desire for peace,' he said laughing.

Joining the laughter and nodding his head in agreement, the doctor got up. Naseema grabbed his shoulder bag and followed him. Ganeshan remembered that she rarely used the car or the scooter these days and mostly relied on public transport. She had already left Saathi and was not a regular in the magazine's office.

They had met on a train journey. A long one that lasted two days and two nights. Naseema was travelling with her parents, and Ganeshan on his own. As it happens in a compartment with just four berths, they started talking and exchanging food and books. Naseema's father was a senior army officer, a brigadier in the Army Medical Corps, while her mother was a professor in microbiology. She herself was a student. Ganeshan had just started his life as a journalist after getting a degree in physics with gold medal. Hearing that, Naseema's mother grew curious, and this also drew Naseema into the conversation. While the mother talked with him about science, the daughter wanted to know more about journalism.

That fateful acquaintance grew into a friendship, first through phone calls, then by letters and meetings. Her parents had no objection to the marriage. And there was no one in Ganeshan's family to object. Three or four years later, Naseema's father died in an accident when hc was on an inspection tour in forward areas. Her mother continued in her research career for a few more years. She had a heart attack while she was in the lab and died on the spot. With no family or pcrsonal moorings as such, their married life sailed ahead smoothly and pleasantly till fate finally decided to take revenge.

Although it happened gradually, Aman disappeared from their conversations, a consequence of the habits and lifestyle they adopted following Aman's death. Ganeshan initially thought of telling her about the notes and poems he had found in Aman's room but then decided against the idea, for fear of bringing back emotions difficult for her to revisit. Her newfound interest in the Nityananda Ashram ruled it out completely.

Naseema's agitation over the stones in the basket sounded unusual to Ganeshan. It didn't go with her nature. So was this inclination towards spirituality. But then he dismissed all that with a smile. The doctor had asked what was wrong if something could bring peace and happiness to the mind. Putting away all thoughts of the morning events, he began to think about the early days of their life together and the two years they were in love prior to their marriage. How they grew closer and closer through brief exchange of words and small incidents. Mentally, then physically. The first time they kissed. Their honeymoon trip to a small island town that was connected with the mainland only by a causeway. How they walked by the tall walls of a fort built by the island's Portuguese rulers, 'with black stones of authority bound in the mortar of fear,' as she described it, watching the violent waves of the sea lashing at its foot. How their salt-soaked bodies had sunk into each other as the wind blew in a chill from the sea—

The telephone rang. It was police inspector Tarun Kumar. He had learnt about Ganeshan's visit to Ashaniketan. Although Ganeshan was surprised, he didn't ask how he found out. The officer asked him if he had found any worthwhile clue.

'Why are you taking that note so seriously, officer?' Ganeshan asked him. 'It is certainly strange that my name was found in the boy's bag. But there can be a dozen reasons for that.'

'Of course. I also think there is nothing in it. I just asked since you had been there. I actually called you for something else.'

Ganeshan waited for him to continue.

'A man with a big cartel of explosives was arrested by the police near the bus terminal yesterday. There is a well-known dhaba near the place they nabbed him. Interrogation has revealed that he belonged to the NGO that manages the children's home.'

'I read the first part of what you said in the paper, but its connection with the NGO was not reported. What has this incident got to do with the killing of that boy by another inmate?'

'It was not just an excess by another inmate. The management is not without faults, it seems, sir. You must have read that the manager has also been arrested.'

'Yes, I did, but what about the explosives?'

'Hmm, could be a coincidence. Sorry to have disturbed you in the morning. Good day to you!'

He placed the receiver back on the cradle, not fully satisfied with the inspector's reply.

Tarun Kumar didn't seem like a fool to Ganeshan. Why did he call him up in the morning to share this news? There seemed to be something more to it than he revealed. Did he knowingly send him Shankar's photo of instead of Vijay's?

The police had given the same photo to the newspapers as well. The fact that three pages of the register containing details of boys who were dead or missing were with him was enough to implicate Ganeshan in this mess. Cawasji's argument was that he had torn the pages out as a way of hollowing out the institutional structure. But a portion of its physical structure had also come down. Why did Cawasji entrust those pages to him? Whatever the reason, Ganeshan was not ready to part with them now. There was no question of going back from it. He had to forge ahead. To where, how and for what purpose, these were the things that had to be figured out.

TWENTY-THREE

With such questions behind him, Ganeshan was again driven to Aman's room, his table and its drawer. Every time he went there, he hesitated a moment before touching the papers. He did not know whether it was hesitation or fear.

The other thing that bothered him was the order of the sheets. Although he was careful to not disturb the order they were in when he discovered them, he had a feeling that he was violating their privacy in some way. Or his mind kept telling him that the order he was so carefully preserving had no order at all. Chronology need not be the only criterion to arrange things. There could be several criteria to do that. The length of the piece, whether it was a poem or something else, Aman's way of liking or valuing them, or some other criterion that was not yet, and perhaps never will be, known to him.

It was a poem this time:

A window pulled itself out of the wall,
The wall on which it had been sitting

Ever since it had become a window.
Those who lived in the room on this side
Had been viewing the same ground through it.
Different people, of course,
Different generations and occupants
But the ground all the same.
Different faces of the ground, of course,
Soaked in rain, shivering in cold
Or aflame in the sun,
Shrouded in shade or eclipsed at night.
They saw trees shedding leaves,
And new ones sprouting, blossoming.
Children playing, beggars fighting for leftovers:
Scenes hosted by the ground all the same.
The viewers were limited to the occupants of a room,
And the scenes not seen yet were countless.
Outworn and dispirited,
The window decided to quit
And bid goodbye to the wall.
The wall decided what was to be seen,
And decreed whom to see.
It went and sat on the road, in the bazaar,
At the border of the country, in the battlefield,
In the houses of whores, in asylums of lunatics,
In jails and in temples,

In the coveted gallery before gallows,
In the noisy durbar of kings,
In the silent burial ground
So that more scenes could be seen,
More people could see through it.
Matches and competitions,
Dances, parties and festivals,
Deceptions and betrayals,
Barters and deals,
Pangs of birth and the ecstasy of mating,
Rapes, murders, arsons, wars,
Kafilas of the displaced,
Jesus crucified,
Nonbelievers burnt,
Jews gassed,
Gypsies hung from the branches of trees,
The toes of slaves chopped off
So they don't run away.
But no one looked through the window
Since there was no wall around it,
It was the wall that defined
Whom to see, who would see and
how much to see.
What could not be seen
Defined what would be seen.

Ganeshan moved the sheet to the bottom of the pile, pushed the drawer close and went to stand near the rear window which opened to the vacant plot of land. The vacant land, shrubs and little flowers, yellow and violet; everything as it was. Since winter had withdrawn, the colour and character of sunlight had changed. Leaving the rear window, he moved to the front one and looked down. The light thrown from it on the yard at night, or the open shutters during the day used to fill his mind with reassurance, 'Yes, the boy was there.' The window allowed him to feel Aman's presence; it was as if the channel through which his silent dialogue with Aman took place. Occasions of their meeting face to face and conversing were so rare. That day…

It was a day like any other. In the morning, Aman came down the stairs, looked at him with a smile and wished him a happy birthday. Nonplussed, having forgotten it was his birthday, Ganeshan looked around. Perhaps, Naseema too didn't remember it. He called Naseema. 'Listen, Naseema, Aman says today is my birthday.'

'July sixteenth, why yes, it is!' she exclaimed.

He felt happiness like he had never experienced on any birthday before. It was with that feeling of lightness that he went to office and returned home.

In the evening, a colleague of Ganeshan and his wife visited them, without notice. Ganeshan and Naseema had no custom of observing or celebrating birthdays. They used to remember their wedding anniversary but then that too fell out of memory during days of adversity. They thought their friends, too, had not kept track of such occasions in their lives, but a friend showed up that day, perhaps to join in their happiness of Aman's return. In a few minutes, Ahuja the merchant navy officer and his wife also arrived. They had no knowledge of the birthday and learnt of it only when his office friend told them. Naseema returned shortly after them; with her was a Saathi friend Shamsher who also happened to be a stage artist. Then it was Colonel Desouza's turn who came over seeing the crowd. Gradually, it developed into a party, in celebration of Aman's return rather than Ganeshan's birthday. Naseema quickly cooked some food and ordered a few things from a restaurant. Ganeshan brought out some whisky to which the colonel supplemented from his stock.

As the night advanced, one by one the guests took leave. The office friend and his spouse were the first to leave, followed by the Ahujas. The colonel and Shamsher sat for some more time, talking. The war memoirs of the colonel interested Shamsher. Then, they too left. Naseema excused herself as she was exhausted. Alone, Ganeshan stood in the veranda and watched the rain suddenly descend from the sky in the silent night.

Aman was upstairs. The lit window in his room meant he was still not asleep. He had came home late. On his way up, he greeted everyone and went to his room. He didn't join the party of the elders.

Some time passed, and he started playing the guitar—it was soft and just audible over the sound of the rain. It went on for a few minutes, then stopped. Everything went quiet. His room was still lit when Ganeshan retired to his bed. Sleep didn't come immediately—he lay in bed watching the block of light from Aman's window falling on the yard and drops of rain falling on it...

It suddenly dawned on him that the only occasion he had heard Aman playing the guitar to an audience was at the dhaba near the bus terminal, the same one where the police had caught someone with explosives. Yet another coincidence! Ganeshan decided to go to the dhaba once again. He remembered the lines of the song Aman and his band had sung that day for quite some time after the event but lost it somewhere down the line. His efforts to recall it later did not succeed.

TWENTY-FOUR

There was something mysterious about this dhaba at least as far as the rumours were concerned. Not far from the busiest bus terminal of the city, it was positioned on the side of the highway. Externally, it was nothing more than an ordinary wayside dhaba offering cheap food and wooden charpoys for resting. As in all roadside dhabas, the customers were mainly truck drivers who wanted to refresh or to break for a night in their long haul. What made it popular was perhaps its proximity to a spacious ground used by the government and public for various purposes.

The slightly elevated land strewn with stones and shrubs was where the government usually put up relief camps when people flowed into the city displaced by natural calamities like floods or communal and ethnic strife in neighbouring localities. Since one problem or the other always haunted the city, the ground would rarely remain empty for long. Again, rumour had it that the crowd was sprinkled with not an insignificant number of foreigners who were apparently also thrown out of their own countries. There was no proper demarcation between the dhaba and the ground and hence a sort of no man's land had come into existence between the two. It was believed that the owner of the dhaba functioned as an unofficial agent when government action was not forthcoming, as it usually didn't, to the camp men, especially outsiders to get their papers ready, establish contacts etc. To what extent he would do that out of human consideration or personal gain could not be said. Interestingly, if he had been indulging in any unauthorised activities, it had not irked any local government officials, for no action had ever been taken against him. In the meanwhile, the dhaba built a reputation for being a place where one could see people of various cultural marks and identities. People came, pitched their own tents, raised hearths, sang songs and danced into the night.

Driven by curiosity and not out of duty, which anyway didn't extend to such matters in his case, Ganeshan had made a visit to the place once, while in service. He wanted to make sure that no one recognised him there and hence had gone alone one evening.

The streetlamps had just been switched on. Some cars had the headlights on while others had not yet turned on the night mode. Since he did not want to draw attention to himself, he left his car at the parking lot of the bus terminal and walked the rest of the way.

The lamps were already on in the dhaba. The eating place had just started filling up. The so-called no man's land was, however, fairly occupied by a myriad crowd, apparent from their detectable quirks and mannerisms and ways of talking. The tents yonder were also in different clusters. Someone was beating the drum and a group of men and women were dancing.

Ganeshan moved through the rows of benches in the eating place. It was an open shed with no cover on any side. The cooking, as usual, happened outside, at the entrance, in full view of the visitors. A man was making rotis and putting them on the inside walls of the red-hot tandoor. Another was taking out the ones that were done with a long iron bar. Vegetables and meat curries were boiling in kadhais adjacent to the tandoor.

Suddenly, the sound of the saxophone rose from somewhere outside. Ganeshan noticed that there was a sort of make-shift platform in place. A boy in jeans and a t-shirt sporting a small beard was standing on it, blowing into the instrument without any accompaniment. The sound of the saxophone was strange to hear in that environment but gradually a small crowd gathered around him and started dancing to it in their own way. Nothing with music and rhythm was alien to the wilderness of the rootless, Ganeshan realised.

As the saxophonist ended his performance and got off the stage, a few boys, five or six of them, got on. As soon as they took position, Ganeshan realised that it was Aman's band, if it could be called that. Ganeshan ducked behind others to hide. The song was:

Gaon ka gussa der se utarta hai
Shahron ki chusti uthtehi gir jati hai*

Bands often borrowed songs by others. The lines impressed him, and he imagined the original was written by some known songwriter. The possibility that it was their own did not occur to him.

A man standing next to him, a lorry driver perhaps, remarked upon hearing the song, 'These people reach this place after journeying for weeks. Men, women, children all, with only fatigue, pain and hunger for company. Many of them must have lost their dear ones. How good that there are at least some boys like these to cheer them up!'

'Why do they play instruments so alien to them?' Ganeshan asked.

'Kids of the city, you know. Shahron ki chusti!' The man then became serious. 'One can offer only what one has. These boys know only these instruments. The people also know that, and they appreciate it. When the boys leave late in the night, they take out their own instruments. One remarkable thing is, however hard and tedious their journey is, they make sure to carry with them their musical instruments.'

---

*When the village rages, it takes ages to die down; When the city flares up, it rarely ever keeps up

Ganeshan felt some comfort in his heart when he left the place. As the truck driver said, it was good that there were some such boys. Besides that, he did not give much thought to it. He made sure that he was not spotted and sneaked out when the performance ended.

TWENTY-FIVE

It was not the same Ganeshan today, and he had no need now to be incognito. Besides, it was not an idle trip now, he was carrying with him an unease that something unusual would occur this time as well. People made to suffer become carriers of hate. Every new day added more friction in relationships between people. In spite of all such possibilities, something kept nagging him that he should have gone there earlier.

The picture of the dhaba had not changed a bit. Everything was in the same shape and place as they were four years ago. The shed, the tables, benches and tandoor, all of it. The sun had already set, and the evening was quietly surrendering to the clutches of darkness. How many people who have lost their homes must have passed through this place in these years! Some must have become part of the city and some might still be holding out, unwilling and resisting to surrender.

Ganeshan occupied a vacant table. It was not yet time for dinner, and the tables were mostly vacant. The ground outside was however not short of people. A difference he noticed was that there were fewer children among them. Had they abandoned their children at the time of escape? Had they come to the city as a people without a new generation? These were not comfortable questions to ask.

No one came to attend to him immediately. Ganeshan was in no hurry as he had no agenda. For a moment he wondered what it was he wanted there. The answer came soon. A boy approached, in dirty clothes, a sweater with holes in it, dusty hair, and a piece of rag on his shoulder with which to clean the tables. Ganeshan asked for rotis and a side of vegetables. He grew a little suspicious as the boy turned to go and called him back. He wanted to take a good look at his face, so he told him that the table was not properly clean and that he should wash his hands before serving. The boy's face resembled one he had seen in the photos from Ashaniketan. Especially, a cut on his chin, which pulled the muscles of his chin upwards on one side, same as the one in the photograph.

When the boy returned with the dishes, there was no doubt on his mind that he had seen that face in one of the photographs. Only which photo, he wondered. It was not the one the police officer had tendered as that of Vijay, which was attached to the page of the register with Shankar's name on it. This boy resembled one of the other two. Gopal, Shankar or Vijay himself? Names had already lost their mooring to persons.

When the boy turned to leave after serving the food, Ganeshan called him from behind, 'Shankar, er, Vijay, I want some more water.'

The boy instantly turned back and said, 'In a moment, sir.'

He stopped after a few steps and turned back to him, 'What did you call me, sir?'

'Your name. You told me when I came here two weeks back, you know.'

The boy stared at him and to Ganeshan's discomfort, he saw fear in those eyes.

'Two weeks back? I gave you my name?'

'Yes, of course.'

'My name is not Shankar.'

'Certainly. You are Vijay, I remember.'

'You are mistaken, sir. I came here only three days ago.'

'But you responded when I called you.'

'Please, sir. Please don't…'

'I am a friend of Vijay's. I won't harm you.'

Ganeshan saw a trace of trust appear in his fearful eyes. 'My name is neither Shankar nor Vijay. I am Shukur.'

'Okay, Shukur, if you prefer. But why are you—'

'Shukur!' the manager called him. 'Go attend to the table on the right corner.'

The boy dashed to the table, in relief. Ganeshan took a mouthful of roti with vegetables and chewed idly. His mind was agitated, perhaps to the same degree as that of the boy's. The dining table and the bizarre city beyond it seemed to have disappeared from his sight. It was now a small world, of a boy and himself, and neither knew how to proceed.

'Anything else, sir?' Shukur was back.

'Please—' said Ganeshan this time, but he could not find more words to go on.

From the conversation between them in the following moments, it became apparent that Shukur and his brother Imtyaz had run away from their strife-stricken village in the north two years ago. All other members of their family had been killed, some by extremists and others by the police. After coming to the city, Shukur lost his brother, too, in a crowded street. Shukur himself ended up within the walls of Ashaniketan, as Shankar. Having escaped from there now, his sole aim was to locate his brother.

'How are you going to do that?' asked Ganeshan.

'There are people who help.'

'Are there such people?'

'I escaped because there are.' Shukur seemed to have no doubt in his mind.

'Who helped you?'

'Another boy, Vijay. He, too, must have got out by now. That was the plan. First myself and then he, following the same procedure. We were to meet here.'

'My God!' Ganeshan exclaimed.

He didn't want to tell the boy anything more, not at the moment. Pressing his hand and assuring him that he would visit again, he hurriedly walked out. There was only one thought that filled his mind. How fragmented is this world! And yet between these fragments, like a boat cruising through an archipelago, he saw one idea making its way. 'There are people who help.' He wondered, was he one of them?

TWENTY-SIX

The newspaper headline said, 'One more wall collapses. No one hurt'. Yet another wall of the Ashaniketan barracks had collapsed! Ganeshan was more shocked the second time he received the news. Cawasji must have torn off some more pages from the register was his first thought. As soon as he thought of it, he felt ashamed. How could his mind subscribe to such illogical nonsense? But wasn't that what he had said? The safest way of dismantling an inhuman set up?

Well, logic appeared to be missing from it all. Once Ganeshan returned from the dhaba, he lined up the torn pages from the register and tried to make sense of what he saw. The photo of the boy he had just met, if Shukur was his name, was stuck on the page titled Gopal. Of course, Vijay's photo, the boy who was killed, was on Shankar's page. But then, didn't Shukur say he was known as Shankar in Ashaniketan? And who was the child labelled as Vijay on the register?

If Cawasji had not torn off Gopal's page by accident, Ganeshan would never have found Shankar alias Shukur or whatever his name was! Ganeshan was grateful for this mistake and he was now, unbelievably so, grateful for this act of violence committed on the register by Cawasji.

Cawasji's intention was to destroy the accounts kept by the children's home, but the records of that place were so defaced and corrupted that anyone who tried to destroy it would just be lost in its labyrinth. That they could make a dent in the account, even if through luck, was itself satisfying.

Ganeshan dialled the phone with the papers still in his hand. Cawasji as usual reacted, 'That is a good thing, isn't it?'

'But Cawasji…' Ganeshan fumbled.

'Don't you get unnecessarily exercised, Ganeshan. Come to my place in the evening if you are free. We shall have a game.'

'I don't want to play any games, Cawasji. I want to talk to you about something important.'

'We will talk about whatever you want, but with a game. I will wait for you.'

When Ganeshan reached Cawasji's house in the evening, he was just dismissing his assistants. Having done that, he pushed the sliding door, letting the office open into the drawing room. He set the table, chessboard and two glasses of whisky. Then he went inside and came back with two more pages of the register and promptly handed them over to Ganeshan. This exchange was becoming something of a routine, Ganeshan feared, much like joining the rooms, setting the board and pouring whisky into glasses whenever they met. Reservations aside, Ganeshan took them almost with eagerness.

'Haltingly though, things are moving. Don't you think so?' asked Cawasji.

'I am thoroughly confused now,' said Ganeshan.

'Clear and stainless, that is an idealised state. Can we afford to wait for such a state?'

'No, but I am talking about those children.'

'Yes, there are so many of them. An equal number of pages in the register, too,' Cawasji said arranging the pawns on the board. 'What would you choose, black or white?'

'You are generalising things, Cawasji,' Ganeshan said without paying attention to the board. 'I am worried about those two particular children. The situation is such that if you untie one knot, four more appear.'

Cawasji chose the white pieces and opened the game by moving the pawn two positions before the king. And then, without taking his eyes off the board, commented on Ganeshan's remark, 'What appear as knots, if you look at them from another angle, could be challenges.'

Mechanically, Ganeshan moved his pawn, too.

Cawasji followed with another pawn on the bishop's line. 'Each move is actually an alternative before you. Are you not selecting one alternative out of many available before you when you make a move? What chess offers to a player are alternatives: chess is a game of alternatives. You pick one of the many alternatives and convert it into a move. And that move, in its turn, opens up another set of alternatives.'

'Oh dear, you have nothing else on your mind than the game. However, if I may put it this way, as the game progresses, the choices or alternatives as you call them get steadily reduced. From ten to five, five to three and so on. And every move binds the player tighter and tighter rather than opening up more vistas. If the loser is left with no moves, the winner, too, is left with only one move in the end. Both are thus locked. That is how choices turn into knots.'

'How nicely you have reversed the proposition and correctly, too, I must say!'

Both of them carried on like that, opening and restricting their choices, and taking small sips from their glasses in between. Cawasji played very carefully and Ganeshan often without direction or forethought. Once Cawasji stopped Ganeshan from making a wrong move. Then suddenly he said, 'What was it you said about knots, Ganeshan?'

Ganeshan leaned back into his chair and said, 'Let us take a break.'

'You said it was very important. Sorry, it went out of my mind.' Cawasji sat back in his chair and picked up his glass.

'Guess what I have discovered,' Ganeshan said.

Cawasji looked enquiringly.

'The missing boy of Ashaniketan has been located.'

'Really?'

'Difficult to believe, eh? I myself could not, at first. Firstly, his name is not Shankar, but Shukur. Cawasji, why did you take him to that horrible place? It was an unpardonable act on your part. Do you know what it cost him? His brother.'

Cawasji stared at Ganeshan. 'That is not correct,' he said visibly agitated. 'Believe me, I don't know any such boy. I don't know any of the boys there. My connection with Ashaniketan is about its buildings, not human beings.'

'But you said that you brought him there.'

Cawasji shook his head vehemently. 'I thought you would understand. It was just a trick I played to make them open the register. I just uttered a name, a very common name, Shankar. It worked, that was all.'

'My God!'

Cawasji added apologetically, 'If we had not taken an offensive position, we would not have been able to extract anything from such clay-cold characters there. They are just pieces on the board. Only if we attack will they respond.'

'We haven't been able to extract anything from them. That is the sad fact. We went there to find out about Vijay and how he had known me. Nothing came out—or instead we came out with this boy, Shankar!'

'That is the law, Ganeshan. You set out for one place and reach elsewhere. Where did you find the boy Shankar—or is it Shukur?'

'At the dhaba near the bus terminal. He serves food there. Do you know something? The police officer who visited my house about finding my name in the boy's bag? He called me a couple of days back and told me that a man with some explosives was apprehended by the police around that dhaba. I wonder why he told me all that. However, it is not good news that the police have their eyes on this place.'

Ganeshan decided not to tell Cawasji about the mismatched photos in the pages of the register. He had no interest in the children as individuals. His interest was in the idea of children, imprisoned in such circumstances.

'The police officer seems to be after something particular,' Cawasji said. 'Anyway there is enough for everybody to investigate in this world. And mind you, it is not even necessary that every mystery is solved. In fact, ninety percent of them would remain to see the graves of their investigators.'

'I know that, Cawasji. There won't be a state when the world is free of all mysteries. However, the question here is not of mysteries as such. At some stage of the enquiry, the subject of investigation becomes more than a mystery. Mysteries and wonders are the qualifications you give to things from a standpoint of detachment. Here, I am beyond that stage now. I am invested in this mystery more deeply. The piece of paper the police officer claimed to be have been discovered from Vijay's bag could very well have its origin elsewhere. Perhaps it was planted there by someone or perhaps by himself. And now I, who went looking for Vijay, have turned to looking for Shukur and his missing brother.'

Cawasji poured some more whisky into their glasses.

'Every pawn in chess starts as a mere pawn when the game begins,' he said. 'As the game progresses, each one of them gets locked with others. They start killing and dying for saving the lives of others.'

'You are right there,' Ganeshan said. 'I am worried about this killing and dying—for others. Didn't you tell me that the organisation running Ashaniketan is an outfit of Pappan?'

Cawasji took quite a few minutes and two or three gulps of whisky before he replied. 'You might be thinking that we both are operating on the same plane,' he said. 'In one way we are, but we are on opposite sides. Ashaniketan is a chessboard between the two of us.'

When his eyes met Ganeshan's, he smiled but it was a grave smile.

'And the games you play, do they end in stalemates?'

'Games where one or the other wins or loses are becoming archaic in chess,' he said. 'Rare and extraordinary. You come across them only once in a while. They are epitaphs to the chess of days bygone.'

Cawasji was rarely emotional. This was, Ganeshan thought, one of those rare moments.

They didn't complete the game.

TWENTY-SEVEN

Rishi could only talk about Seeta, about his meeting with her and everything that happened afterwards. Ganeshan was not sure if it was normal for a lover to pour out his thoughts, his emotions so before a friend. Perhaps he was trying to fill the space left by the unpredictabilities in their relationship.

Ganeshan only knew about Seeta from what Naseema and Rishi had told him. Once he had also seen a photograph. She smiled very rarely, Rishi had told him. The smile in the photograph must have been one of those rare gifts. According to Ganeshan, the photograph was nothing special. She looked just like any other girl. He was not sure whether he would recognise her if he met her on the street.

Rishi's love towards the girl oscillated between affection and undaunted respect. They mostly talked over the phone, that too by prior planning. Meetings with her were rare and valuable for him. Ganeshan had once mentioned how people sometimes define a particularly important day as the first day of the rest of their lives. Rishi borrowed that phrase when he talked about the days he got to meet her. But today was different. He seemed particularly anxious about her this time, as if the love between them had somehow taken a backseat.

'I don't know how to convince her,' Rishi said. 'In fact, I never tried. It wouldn't be right. What qualification do I have after all other than that I have lived two or three years more than her? I have not seen the life she has seen. True, that life has become a liability to her. It has made her so desensitised, numb towards everything.' Rishi now knew the numbness she showed towards him was a part of her general apathy to life. She tried to distance herself from all kinds of emotions and relationships that others would value in life.

As a two-year-old girl, abandoned and wandering in the streets, Seeta was spotted by a kind policeman. She had preserved a clear memory of that policeman even after she grew up, according to the couple who became her parents later. 'He gave me only two pieces of chocolate, the rest he kept in his pocket,' she used to tell them. The policeman took her to the station, and then to his home. When no one turned up to claim her, she was finally put in an orphanage. It was perhaps the year and half she spent in that place that insulated her towards human relationships at that young age. The lack of warmth, negligence and the punishments played an important part in making the Seeta Rishi knew. When she was three and a half years old, a childless couple adopted her. In spite of the love and care they showered on her, she could never make it her home or them her parents, they used to say with sadness. The fear in her mind had vanished, but she continued to be reticent with her affection and indifferent to the affection of others. 'Something in her resisted becoming our daughter,' her adoptive parents confessed.

Her apathy towards human relationships did not earn her many friends in school or college, but she showed exceptional brilliance in her studies. The education and training given to her by her step-parents (that was how she referred to them) provided her with the confidence and strength to stand on her feet, she would say without any reservation. Yet when she acquired that strength, she expressed her desire to live independently. They didn't object. Seeta, of course, didn't break her relationship with them. Every Sunday she talked to them over the phone. When they were in town, she would visit them and have lunch with them but she insisted on living separately.

Rishi was sure that Seeta knew that he loved and respected her. He was also certain that she had no closer friend than him, but she didn't encourage their relationship to go further. Not just that, he felt that she was growing more and more introverted. 'She is withdrawing into herself and that makes me anxious,' he said. A person of few words, Seeta was free with only Naseema, who was taken with spirituality at the moment.

Ganeshan didn't have much to offer him in terms of consolation. He said, 'Naseema was telling me that Seeta is planning to join a book publishing firm. She is of the view that Seeta has all the qualities to become a good editor. Editors should be people of few words according to her!'

'And writers babblers? Don't you describe me that way, Ganeshan!'

'I didn't mean it like that, Rishi.'

'Yes, she is trying for a change,' Rishi said, reflecting. 'Would be good for her, although I cannot advise her. If I said something, she would immediately counter me and ask me what was wrong with her present job. She would say she is an independent woman earning her living, why should she bother with whose company it is?'

'Well, that would be correct, wouldn't it, Rishi?'

'No, not in this company. There is an obvious discomfiture between her and her employers, and it is getting worse. I can understand it even if she does not say it. That is why I would be happy if she leaves it. It is not just a company where Pappan puts his money. He has a personal eye over its affairs. He might not know anything about information technology, but he knows how it can be misused, criminally. Just because of that, he has very close watch at every person working there.'

'It was Seeta who told Naseema about Pappan's connection with the organisation running Ashaniketan.'

'It is the nastiest level of Pappan's activities,' said Rishi. 'Not many people know about it—his connection with it and what happens there. And those who know won't talk. Ganeshan, I know Seeta is not happy there—everyone suspects everyone else at their workplace. And I know Seeta, she can't help but say what she feels. Just think why she spilled this to Naseema. Something she doesn't like must have happened. The children in the orphanage are still her anchor. Well, I guess, it is good there is something she cares about...'

TWENTY-EIGHT

'I have to go somewhere. Will you come with me?' Naseema's voice choked as she said that.

She had returned late the previous evening. Ganeshan had dozed off in front of the TV. He knew she must have switched it off. She woke him up and told him to go to bed.

She was up in the morning before him. When he came to the coffee table to fix a cup of tea, she was at the basin gargling with warm water. Soon she joined him for the morning tea. It was then she said that.

'Sure, tell me when you want to go,' he said. 'You seem to have a sore throat. It was a chilly night, may be due to the rain in the evening. Did you get wet? A rain was needed after the oppressive heat.'

'I am all right, Ganeshan. Shall we start after breakfast?'

'Okay with me.'

'A girl who used to be with us at Saathi is not well. Vasundhara.'

'Vasundhara, yes, think I have met her.'

'Quite possible. She used to be at the helm of everything there. Active and intelligent, too.'

'I found her very reasonable. When I had to confront them a couple of occasions,' he remarked with a grin. 'Her conduct differed from the usual activists we met.'

Naseema was not delighted. She sounded sad when she said, 'Rational was a qualification that suited Vasundhara more than reasonable. A bit too rational, more than required. That was her undoing I think.'

Naseema was leading to something. Ganeshan furrowed his forehead. 'What has happened to her?'

'No one knows what exactly happened. It is a mental problem, Ganeshan. Schizophrenia, according to the doctors.'

'My goodness!'

'For a month or so now,' Naseema continued. 'She is also turning violent sometimes, they say. She is on medication.'

Naseema opened up more in the car. Vasundhara had been in a team of committed social workers called Maitri, consisting of a doctor, a journalist and her. According to them, disease was a product of the way of life of the people, shaped by the social, political and economic forces of society. Conscious of the inadequacies of the western-oriented hospital-based healthcare system, the inequitable distribution of health services and inappropriateness of medical education in dealing with the health problems of the majority in the country, they started a project called *Participating Health*. Their first step was to prepare a comprehensive guidebook for educating health workers and giving them a sense of direction. Prepared with a large number of illustrations, charts, questions and answers and anecdotes, the work captured instant attention and was acclaimed as an extremely useful book for everyone from attendants to doctors. Even when she was fully preoccupied with the project, she used to come to Saathi on Sundays and in the evening on other days. She was initially living with an aunt of hers. Then she became close with a theatre artist named Shamsher. 'You might remember him, he has come to our house once. A good friend of Saathi,' said Naseema.

'Of course, I remember. A tall fair fellow with a well-trimmed salt-and-pepper beard.'

'Yes. She lived with him for some months. Then they broke up for some reason. She didn't go back to her aunt, instead took a one room apartment near her house and lived there alone. Once the book project was over, Maitri workers moved out to a distant rural area, to try their ideas on the ground. Vasundhara didn't accompany them. She continued to come to Saathi, but a kind of withdrawal or loneliness became apparent in her behaviour. She frequently quarrelled with her friends on trivial issues.'

'Who is with her now?'

Her aunt visits. Then someone or the other from Saathi would be there. She wants someone from Saathi with her at all times.'

Vasundhara was sleeping when they reached her place. A girl called Rajani was with her. As they talked, Vasundhara woke up. She washed her face and came and sat with them. The effect of the drugs was visible in her sleepy eyes and swollen face. She wished Ganeshan and Naseema in an emotionless voice. She briefly talked about the hospital and her treatment. Then she herself asked Rajani for her medicine. Her aunt, who had come by then, prepared some tea. With the tea, Vasundhara came and sat beside Naseema, and held her hand. Naseema, like an elder sister, patted her back and touched her cheeks. Vasundhara showed no emotion but said rather mechanically, 'Find some time to come here.'

Naseema assured her she will. Vasundhara closed her eyes and seemed to be relapsing into a nap.

They didn't talk much on their way back. Naseema expressed fear that Saathi was breaking up. In the absence of Vasundhara it might suffer more, she felt. She also indicated that she herself was not going there.

'That is the law,' Ganeshan added rather philosophically. 'Breaking up in one place to create somewhere else. Even when we feel things are getting irretrievably fragmented, there might be aquifers underneath helping join the pieces together.'

'Who can comment on human character?' Naseema went on. 'Vasundhara was of a dominating nature, but everyone loved her. Rajani was especially close to her. A girl on the brink of suicide who came to Saathi for refuge, she grew into a committed and resolute worker just because of Vasundhara.'

Meeting Ganeshan's inquisitive eyes, she said, 'I will tell you about it some other time.'

They drove silently. When they reached a relatively quiet area, Naseema said. 'Let us stop here and walk for some time.'

The sun had started setting. Rains the day before had made the weather a bit pleasant. They were on a wooded pathway that provided ample shade, but one had to frequently go around the giant trees. Both sides of the road were bordered with large houses with wide yards and gardens. They walked silently, lost in their selves.

'You are upset,' Ganeshan said.

'Yes. If there is any place of worship around, we could go in for a few moments.'

They walked looking for such a place and soon spotted one. It was a Christian church. It was not prayer time and its premises were empty. Only the vicar's house at the back showed some activity. The prayer hall was open, and they stepped in. Naseema sat on a bench and closed her eyes. She was in need of spiritual nourishment. Ganeshan sat by her side for a while and then stepped out. He walked along the neat, gravelled path outside, listening to the sound of his steps. Bordering the green lawn were beds of rose, lily and jasmine.

After some time, Naseema, too, came out. They walked back and got into the car.

'Is it necessary to remove from our mind things we have lost?'

'Will the mind obey attempts to remove?'

She ignored his comment and said, 'I think faith is not a thing that rubs out feelings of loss. It only converts them into a form acceptable to us.'

'What kind of faith are you talking about?'

'Faith, faith in something. In concepts, in men, maybe in life itself.'

Again, they fell silent.

TWENTY-NINE

It was many days later that Naseema told Ganeshan about Rajani. One day, he had taken out the copy of *Participating Health* from Naseema's shelf and dusted it.

The first section of the book followed the thoughts and experiences of a nurse in a city hospital. Six months after she qualified as a nurse, the matron, pleased with her work, asked her to be the sister-in-charge of a ward. She was excited and proud and wanted to continue in the hospital. However, she had to look after her ailing mother in the village, so she sought a job nearer to her place and started working at a rural dispensary. The question discussed here was why people in villages didn't understand that it was for their own good to get treated early. Through a discussion on what is disease as opposed to illness, the authors proceeded to the next question: Why do people have faith in local healers? Ganeshan came across this statement: Villagers see illness as punishment given by God for falling out of harmony with the universe. What local healers did, according to them, was detect where the harmony was broken and in effect correct it. For that, they took the help of spirits and souls of the departed.

Ganeshan found himself confronted with a question. If it is God who punishes them for the rupture in harmony, why would people seek the help of spirits for rectifying it? Why are souls of the dead commissioned to correct disharmonies in the lives of the living? Vasundhara's dull and heavy face, asking for medicines from Rajani, came to his mind. How different it was from the bright and lively face that he remembered from earlier! Was it the medicine or her illness? At some point in her life, Vasundhara seemed to have broken her harmony with the universe.

Naseema walked in. She sat down and started telling him about Rajani.

Rajani was very close to ending her life when she had reached Saathi. Naseema was in office at the time and she remembered her narrating her story. As a schoolgirl, she was attracted to a young neighbour. He said he was a salesman and after every sortie into the city, he would bring her attractive presents. Their love grew, and her girlish infatuation forced her to run away with the youth, against the advice and warning of her parents. They started living in a small rented house in the city. Their love was deep and genuine, but suddenly the whole edifice they had built collapsed. One day, when the man was away, the police raided their house and took away all they had. She was shocked to learn that her husband was a thief, and they were living on wealth accumulated through thievery. When he returned at night, she berated him, calling him a thief and a cheat and all other words that came to her mind. She beat him with a stick and threw him out. He received everything silently without uttering a word in defence. In the morning, when she opened the door, she saw her husband hanging from a tree in the yard.

It was unbelievable the way Vasundhara had patiently and steadily worked on this traumatised girl of tender age and moulded her into a cheerful and resolute worker of the organisation. It was one of the wonders in the annals of Saathi.

'Do you think Rajani would be able to reclaim Vasundhara in the same manner?'

'There are wonders in life, but not so much mathematical equilibrium,' said Naseema, looking into distance.

'I was telling you the other day that beneath the cracked earth there are aquifers flowing, helping join the pieces together without our knowledge. They continue to flow. Call them Vasundhara or Rajani or by some other name…'

'God?'

'God, Satan, what one calls it does not matter. Imagination does.'

THIRTY

'How many artists are needed in a band?' Ganeshan asked Rishi while driving.

'Pop music does not have any hard rules. It became *pop* by rebelling against rules, if I understood it correctly. Any number of participants, any instrument can make it work.'

'You are right.'

Ganeshan recited a few lines:

Don't you choose your instrument
Use the one you have
Don't worry about the tenor and timbre
Time will take care
Don't get stuck on the lyrics
Allow the mood to weave them.

'What is that?' asked Rishi, raising his eyebrows.

'I read them somewhere.' Ganeshan tried to swallow his words.

In fact, those words were etched on Ganeshan's mind. Like a credo, Aman had written them on the centre of a page. He had some doubt about the last line. If lyrics had to be woven according to the mood of the occasion, why did he compose so many of them? But that question was answered on another page. Again in the centre of a page, like the title of the whole collection: 'Songs to try/tried'. All were perhaps not written in advance. What was sung at the spur of the moment was perhaps copied on the paper later, at least in some cases.

'Ganeshan, there is something on your mind,' Rishi pressed.

'A long way back, one evening I had gone to this dhaba we are going to now,' he said. 'I had gone out of curiosity from all the stories I had heard about the place. There I saw a few boys, a band if you will, playing the guitar and singing amidst people camping on the grounds. Aman was in the band. He didn't see me. For some reason, I thought he shouldn't see me there so I hid among the crowd and left abruptly. After that, I visited the place only last week. There was no band then. But I saw Shukur in the dhaba. Shukur, also known as Shankar.'

Cawasji was not interested in Vijay, Shankar or Shukur but Ganeshan was, so for his private investigation, he made Rishi his partner. Thus, on an overcast afternoon in the rainy season, the two set out to the dhaba.

To his disappointment, Shukur was not there. Taking their seats on one of the benches lying scattered there, Ganeshan and Rishi kept scanning the whole area.

'What does Shukur look like?' Rishi enquired.

'Medium height, around fifteen. He has a thin frame and a cut on the lower chin. The muscles of the chin appear to have drawn up due to the wound—I have a photo.'

Ganeshan took out Gopal's page from the Ashaniketan register and folded it in such a way that only the photo could be seen and held it up to Rishi.

The boy who came up to take their order was younger than Shukur. He had no knowledge of any boy called Shukur or Shankar.

'This boy, too, could have a terrible history behind him as the one we are looking for,' Rishi reflected. 'His life, too, could be such a dark hole, a deep mine with only heat and no oxygen.'

Ganeshan looked at him silently.

'I am sorry,' said Rishi. 'I didn't mean it. I was thinking of how mines are connected through shafts, and you move from one to another…Here comes the boy with our food. Let us try him once more.'

'Babuji, we boys are like the customers who come here,' said the boy as he arranged the plates. 'We come and go. How many names can one remember! Next time you come, I may not be here.'

'Where will you go from here?'

The boy shrugged and started to leave. Then he turned back and said, 'Why don't you ask the malik?'

Figuring that might be the right course, Ganeshan and Rishi finished their food and approached the manager at the counter. He didn't at all look like the person he was made out to be in the stories knit around the place. Slightly plump with a small tummy, and thick moustaches drooping down at the ends, he had a cheerful air about him. He was sitting at the table, one hand supporting his chin, enjoying the breeze of the pedestal fan. He welcomed them with an open smile.

Instead of Shukur, Ganeshan asked him about the boys of the pop band who used to perform there.

'Band? That band has been disbanded, babuji. Those boys are not seen here these days. All gone their different ways.'

Clearing his throat, Ganeshan asked if he knew how that happened.

'How do all these things happen?' He drew a half circle with his chin pointing at the people camping in the ground. 'No reason, babuji. Things just happen.'

Encouraged by the better reception he received, Ganeshan said, 'I knew one of those boys.'

As soon as he said that, he regretted it. He felt guilty of degrading Aman just as someone he knew.

'Imtyaz, was it?' The manager asked.

Imtyaz, Shukur's brother, was in Aman's band? Ganeshan felt excited. He could have seen him then. Imtyaz could even have visited his home with Aman.

'Yes, Imtyaz.'

'They lost the boy.' There was sadness in his voice. 'He was kidnapped. There is no rhyme or reason to things these days. One can understand children of rich people being kidnapped. Who will pay ransom for ones like Imtyaz? Fools. There was also a white man with Imtyaz when he was kidnapped, people say. The man had apparently come to learn Indian music. He even sang here one day with those boys. The two of them had gone to the hills for a break. They were taken on the way. Neither have been traced. It was a big blow to the boys. An extremely lovable boy he was, Imtyaz. In fact, all of them were so. Boys no one could help but be fond of. And mind you, all of them had a past of suffering and hardship, but they were not brought down by despondency. Surprisingly, a boy called Shukur came here and was with us for some days. Wretched fellow came looking for Imtyaz who he said was his brother. I didn't tell him about Imtyaz's fate. Didn't have the courage, babuji. I told him that the band had been disbanded. Hoping that the band would again come together one day, he stayed on. Now he, too, has disappeared.'

Everything you managed to reach and grasp slips away. Every stream you try to follow dries up midway. In Aman's papers, there were no phone numbers or addresses or even the names of his friends. All that he had left was one group photo. One of them could be Imtyaz. A boy looking down at him from the wall was kidnapped, another was dead. Like notes of music crashing into each other, the whole band seemed to be crashing, too, by kidnappings, deaths and disappearances. If music could survive on a muted frame, it must look like that photo. All the notes and notations were there, yet the music lay outside.

Rishi placed his hand on Ganeshan's shoulder. Suddenly from the tents the sound of a drum rose. Everyone's attention was drawn to it.

'They are from the east,' the manager said. 'There is not much further to go westwards. They themselves don't know which direction they are headed. This is a place where directions end. All that is left with them, representing the place they came from, is a few songs and their musical instruments. They carry their past in them. If hope is God, they have lost their gods. People don't like to admit that their gods have forsaken them, so instead they say their gods have been stolen. The boys were perhaps helping them reconnect with their gods. Their music was different from everyone else's. I don't know whether it worked. No one knows.'

The drummer came out in the open and started beating faster. As he did so, a few other drummers joined him. They played as they liked, not caring to achieve a common rhythm.

The sky darkened, and a breeze raised dust into the air. The drums assumed a fierce rhythm and the drummers, as if possessed, one after the other leapt into the air with their instruments, revolving and landing over and over. They were, however, not experts in the art of acrobatics. Their beats and steps erred and as they landed on the ground, very often they fell down, sometimes on their sides. But they got up, did it again, to fail and fall again. It was certainly not a show of skills, only an exhibition of emotions they could not contain within themselves. Whether they found relief or not, their bodies were certainly hurt in the act.

'Doesn't it look like an art performance?' said the manager who had stood up and was watching, with everyone else. 'But this is just life, their life.'

It started raining and before long, it turned into a heavy downpour. The drummers were not in a position to get up from where they fell. The rain poured over them, cementing them with mud. Their friends came and lifted them and carried them back to the tents. The performance ended without a conclusion or applause.

The manager returned to the counter, and Ganeshan and Rishi to their seats. There was nothing to do there, but they were not in a hurry to leave and sat silently watching the rain.

It was then that inspector Tarun Kumar made his appearance. After folding his umbrella and shaking off the water from his shoes, he straightened and looked around.

Ganeshan pointed him out to Rishi. 'I wonder what he is doing here. Maybe because it was here that they caught a man with a cache of explosives...'

Ganeshan didn't want to get entangled with him here, so he withdrew his eyes.

Rishi kept his eyes on him and said, 'Uhm, Ganeshan, I have a suspicion that he followed you here.'

'Why should he do that?'

'I don't know. But he is watching you. He had spotted you the very moment he came in and then pretended to be looking elsewhere. He is in mufti too.'

'See, he is coming towards us. Our eyes met, now I can't evade him.'

The inspector came up to them and said hello.

'It is a surprise, you eating in a dhaba. We too eat in dhabas often. Our duty is like that, you know. I would say one thing for sure, nothing can beat the taste of dhaba food.'

'Rightly said. Meet my friend Rishi, a writer. He is giving me a dhaba treat.'

The inspector shook his hands.

'Have a seat, Inspector,' Rishi invited him.

'Sorry, I am in a hurry right now. I am following a lead, you know.' The inspector walked away.

Ganeshan said, 'No. He is not after me. Both of us are perhaps after the same person. He must have learnt that a boy called Shankar ran away from Ashaniketan. Locating him without alerting everyone must be important for somebody. He must have figured out that I know something. He gave me a photo of Shankar and called it Vijay's.'

'Suppose he was trying to misguide you?'

'Why should he do that?'

'He might not even be after Shankar. Perhaps someone else.'

'Who? Imtyaz?'

Rishi shook his head. 'If it were Imtyaz, he had no reason to follow you.'

'Then?'

'Aman, for example.'

'Please, Rishi.'

'I am sorry, Ganeshan,' Rishi placed his hand on Ganeshan's. After a while, he added reflectively, 'I think we are all showing off our intelligence.'

Just then, the manager came up to them again.

'Am I disturbing you?' He said politely.

'Not at all,' Ganeshan said. 'You are in one way giving us confidence, a lot of it.'

'Thanks for that. Your interest in music had me thinking that you might be favourably inclined towards other arts also.'

'You have piqued our interest,' said Rishi.

'If you have travelled by road east of Panch Ratan market, you must have come across a railway crossing, a manned one,' the manager began to explain. 'There is an abandoned factory near it.'

'I have seen it,' Ganeshan said. 'It is on the main road itself. I used to wonder why such a large plot was lying unutilised. Some people have encroached on it and put up shacks there.'

The manager laughed. 'Not everywhere,' he said. 'A portion of it has been converted into an art gallery.'

'An art gallery inside an abandoned factory!'

'Difficult to believe? It is also difficult to locate it. From the railway crossing, you have to walk along the tracks. The obscurity prevents most people from reaching it. There are also no advertisements.'

'I will visit it though I am not a connoisseur of art.'

The manager laughed as if to say everyone says so.

'How long would it be there?'

'Till another artist comes up! I know nothing of art. If you find it good, you should tell me.'

'You are…'

'A sponsor you may say.'

The manager went back. The rain had subsided, but the clouds still hung in the sky, and the cool breeze hinted there would be more rains.

Ganeshan and Rishi rose to go.

The people in the tent were active again. This time it was a song, with the accompaniment of a string instrument. Ganeshan saw that they were wearing their traditional long, flowing dress even though it was summer in the city.

THIRTY-ONE

'No one grows up just by sucking their thumb alone,' Rishi argued. 'All of us carry within ourselves the legacy and experiences of our elders and friends. This is truer about artists and writers.'

This was the gist of a middle written by Rishi: A woman jumped into a river to end her life. The river, flowing from one country to another, carried her to the neighbouring country. While the policemen of that country saved her life, they put her in jail for unlawful entry. Her adventure led her to a life more unbearable than the one she wanted to end. Between the endless journeys to courts and back to jails, a constable became close to her and gave her a child. The child became a problem between the married policeman and the prisoner–mother, just as she was a problem for the two countries. When the woman was finally deported back to her country, she didn't want to carry yet another unwanted life with her. The policeman as usual looked the other way. The kid was abandoned on the road.

Rishi said it was a story Seeta and he wove together long back while discussing various problems that arose between two inimical countries. He made a middle piece out of it, but when it came out in print, Seeta went ballistic on him. He had thought that she would be happy to read it. 'She claims that it is her story, and the abandoned child was she herself,' Rishi said.

'Why did I have to do it,' he lamented. 'Could a two-year-old child remember such details?'

She had a profound answer for that: 'The memory of suffering and torture is harder than other memories.'

'Either she is making it up just for the sake of quarrelling with me,' he said, 'or she has started believing stories her imagination weaves. I am sad if it is the former but shudder to think of the possibility of the latter.'

Ganeshan and Naseema sat across the coffee table as he told them about the conversation. Naseema was friends with Seeta, but she, too, had little contact with her now. Seeta had left her job and had joined a publishing company. Naseema did not know the name of the company. All she knew was that it was somewhere outside the city, and Seeta had shifted closer to work. Rishi, too, received only that much information through a phone call.

'We have to locate her,' Ganeshan said. 'I think she is in danger. That is why she has changed her job and residence. And why she is not giving anyone any details.'

'But how Ganeshan?'

'That question, Naseema, is now in everything I am faced with. I am unable to even see what is right in front of me.'

THIRTY-TWO

Aman would have looked at the situation this way:
When they jump from one tree to another
Monkeys might be thinking of
The tree they just left
Or the tree they have yet to catch but not yet caught,
Mostly about the latter.
But they spend some moments
Between two trees.
Anxious moments.
Where will we account for those moments?
Nowhere,
Because it is a gap
Call it a nowhere-space, a discontinuity.
Spaces that do not belong anywhere,
Spaces that could not become something
Spaces that did not become anything.
Breaks,

for them anchors ask for forbearance
Audiences gracefully pardon,
Actors take in their stride.
Breaks,
From them stories come back,
Life joins back
Trees appear.
Monkeys are somewhere, back from nowhere.
When after experiments of ages,
And endless abiding efforts,
To keep continuity
Where campaigns withdraw,
Where philosophies bow out.

THIRTY-THREE

'The idea of home comes out of its collapse.' So says the description of the artist below his painting, of a building lying collapsed in earthquake. Buckled columns, beams slanting, walls and ceilings thrown open by huge holes and doors and windows blocked by fallen objects. The role of each structure is best expressed by its destruction.

The art and the artist Ganeshan met in the abandoned factory were extraordinary.

The eastward road from Panch Ratan market was a busy one. The market, a veritable picture of wealth and prosperity, was however closed that day for the annual remembrance of the trading community's past, steeped in violence and tragedy. A programme was on in the park for members of the community only. It had assumed an air of ritualistic secretiveness over the years. The park was cordoned off on all sides by white sheets, and the entire area wore a gloomy look as every shop was shuttered and even hawkers did not dare trade.

There was a road that ran parallel to the railway tracks, and another that branched out of it, crossing them. The abandoned factory was situated at the juncture. The factory premises started right at the edge of the road with a wall three stories high. It was perhaps the office portion of the complex, the shops lay adjacent to it but were much shorter in height. Roofs with corrugated sheets had developed holes in them; shutters of several windows had fallen off or were detached and precariously hanging from their hinges. Pigeons were flying in and out through the openings. At places, the plaster had fallen off of the walls, revealing naked bricks. The gate was fastened with a double lock and sealed.

Following the advice of the dhaba manager, Ganeshan walked along the railway tracks and entered the compound through an opening in the wall. It was the hole encroachers were using to go in and out of the place like the pigeons above them. There were a few rooms in one block meant for the watch and ward staff. A lavatory block stood behind it. Both were in use by some chowkidars posted to guard the assets. Heaps of scrap metal were gathering rust, and a number of containers were lying in the open. It became evident that the encroachers were not outsiders, but the jobless old workers of the company. They tried to stop Ganeshan but when he mentioned the exhibition, they allowed him in.

Ganeshan walked past silent machines, displaced conveyor belts and hanging wires. Climbing the stairs in the shop building and walking across the expanded metal floor, he reached the office rooms seen from the main road. The gallery was in one of those rooms.

Since there was no electricity, there were no lights and fans. The walls were covered with cobwebs and spiders were busy. The air was sultry. Breeze coming in through the open windows provided some relief.

The artist was the lone human presence inside. A lean man of medium build in pants and a slightly soiled shirt. He did not have a beard but had a shadow worth two or three days. Everything concerning him was so ordinary that Ganeshan thought he could have easily met him and forgotten. Seeing the visitor, he got up from the chair at the window and introduced himself as Koshi. He didn't ask Ganeshan how he happened to visit the exhibition nor did he offer to accompany him. As Ganeshan moved towards the paintings, he returned to his seat by the window. He was working on a painting sitting there, Ganeshan noticed.

It was not an all-painting exhibition. Some were photographs, some collages and some sculptures. There was no proclaimed theme or topic for the show but as he moved from one to another, Ganeshan could not help feel that the show as a whole was a mere continuation of the place in which it was being shown, the broken factory. It was difficult to say where the factory ended and the art began. Ganeshan remembered that the manager of the dhaba didn't answer his question about the strangeness of holding an art exhibition in a broken factory. Collapsed buildings, abandoned habitations, ruins left behind by fire, earthquakes and wars…the show depicted destruction after destruction. He saw reptiles crawling over the debris, now disappearing inside and now surfacing, human bodies fiercely assaulting each other or violently digging into each other in the act of mating, cities so congested and packed with houses that streets had disappeared altogether and streets lit only by window lights, not streetlamps. One painting represented a deserted burial ground under an overcast sky, marked with crosses broken, slanting or fallen down and shrubs growing around them. Refugees making their home inside neglected monuments and grass and shrubs finding a home in the cracks and crevices; kafilas of refugees coming in one direction and caravans of nomads going in the other, both getting entwined spirally like cobras in a mating game… languidness of decaying colonies subjugated by the fury of the dispossessed and the fury of the dispossessed overpowered by the sloth of the nomad…

Ganeshan was specially attracted by the notes and descriptions the artist had left, sometimes below the works or at times, just anywhere. They acted like sorrows and dreams and hopes swimming through spaces left between destruction, loss, absence and deficiencies.

Components of a house: concrete, bricks, glass, space, memory, expectations, presences and absences, said one note.

Houses built between gains and losses, solids and voids, old and new, in which plays of dreams and nightmares, love and hate, procreation and murder are enacted, said another.

Traffic jams of narrow streets created by delays of sadness, breaks of nostalgia, speed of enmity and fear and accidents of encounters and collisions…

Houses are efforts of man to build permanence in the environment of transience and his successes and failures…

It was perhaps the environment of ruin and destruction in the factory that made it not look alien at all. Ganeshan was certainly incapable of providing an interpretation of the works or notes before him. Interestingly, it did not feel like such interpretations would be required.

Ganeshan was a rare visitor, perhaps the only visitor, to the exhibition. But Koshi did not indicate it. From Koshi, Ganeshan learnt that he was an employee of the closed factory. Not just an employee, he had been the leader of the erstwhile union of the workers. Like the exhibition staged there, the artist, too, had been a continuation of the closed factory. The manager of the dhaba, whose name Ganeshan failed to ask, was the manager of the factory, too. When the factory was operational, Koshi had led a number of strikes and clashed with the management. But it appeared both of them had great respect for each other. When the factory closed down, both the management and the union became irrelevant. Both collapsed. Rendered alone, each worker was left to mind his own affairs. Unable to put the factory back on its feet, and under the weight of debt, the manager found another job, strangely in the dhaba.

Locked in disputes, liabilities and cases, the factory and premises fell to a state of disrepair. The reason for the closure of factory was not conflict between workers and management but obsolescence of technology, according to Koshi. It could not stand up against bigger companies and newer technologies. The management started losing grip. Machines had not gone out of service. They had plenty of life left, but it was not possible to make them work profitably.

'Like machines, we too are turning into scrap even with a lot of life left in us, sir,' Koshi said. 'Not because of any deficiency in us, because there are better ones available. Betterness has no moral or philosophical connotations. It only means someone else is falling behind. In fact, values, ideas, philosophies, all face the same threat of falling behind. Everything that fails to keep up-to-date is pushed into the margin and declared as waste, including human beings.'

'Do you think your manager was successful when he took the fight to an entirely different area, to the very margins?'

'I do not know if the word fight has any relevance now. It might be more meaningful if we can get into the cracks that appear everywhere now and then and fill them as far as possible.'

'You have been a leader of the workers.'

'The experience of a century-long association with social values is now trying to tell us that such values do not exist in reality. Society has given up on man. Asking him to carry on his fight alone and individually. Without the help of organisations or ideologies.'

'Have you left the union?'

'There is no leaving. The union has ceased to exist. The union, along with the idea of the union.'

'How did you land in this field, in art?'

'Organisations have resigned and left. A silent explosion has broken up society and thrown up little bits called individuals in the air. One has only himself to explore. When I did that I met this friend of mine, the artist. That he had all along been there was a revelation.'

'I am no connoisseur of art,' Ganeshan said hesitantly. 'In fact, I should claim total ignorance of the subject. Yet, a thought came to mind after seeing your works. That instead of criticising the destruction and fragmentation all around, they seem to be idealising or celebrating it. A friend of mine, an architect, also does it, though at a different level, through his intellectual exercises and symbolic interferences.'

A shadow of sadness fell on Koshi's face. 'You cannot take on a process of such gigantic scale,' he said. 'When I spoke of filling the gaps, I spoke of the immediate necessity. Whether anything else is possible at all, only time can tell. You and I may not live to that point. But the gaps are stretching to assume the proportion of distances, which when it happens will be beyond the capacity of us poor beings to bridge…'

***

While returning home, Ganeshan had a feeling that there were some other people sitting in his car. Vijay, Shukur, Imtyaz, Seeta, Vasundhara, Aman and all his friends…he had not met many of them. Even if he met them somewhere, he would not recognise them. That was, however, not important. Their presence felt so real that he in fact turned and looked at the back-seat. He felt foolish, but he was happy to be foolish.

THIRTY-FOUR

Ganeshan was folding the mosquito net in the morning. Mosquitoes had reappeared after the rains. So every evening the net went up, and every morning it was taken down and folded. Each season has its own rituals. He had switched on the TV as he straightened the bed, and the news came on. Gory pictures of the massacre that had taken place in the city a day before flashed on the screen.

With his eyes on the screen, Ganeshan poured out hot water into the cup and dipped a tea bag into it. He called Naseema from the kitchen.

'I cannot see these things, Ganeshan,' she said. 'It was on yesterday's evening news. You had not returned then. I had to switch it off.'

'Yes, I was delayed. Met some friends at the function in the club so I stayed on for dinner.'

Naseema went back into the kitchen.

After a round of headlines, the newsreader returned to the main story. The incident took place in the evening at a marriage reception. It was a terrorist attack. This was now a new strategy: strike at the most unexpected places where there wouldn't be any security. The aim was of course to create fear. The timing was perfect. The *baarat* was just arriving, and the whole party had crowded at the entrance of the marriage hall to welcome them. Four or five assailants drove in on three motorcycles like a lightning, emptied volleys of rounds from their automatic weapons for a minute or two and then fled. The engines were running, and the shooters did not leave the pillion seats through it all. Women and children happened to be at the frontlines, and they fell over one another. Twenty-five people died on the spot. As they fled, one of the assailants fell down from the bike, and the others shot him too, not to leave any loose ends behind. After presenting the macabre scenes of the bloodbath: the running crowd and the fleeing assailants shot by the wedding videographers, the reader announced the situation was under control in the city and moved on to the next item of news. The trial drama of the dethroned prime minister of the neighbouring country was over: the sentences would be pronounced shortly. That was a staple item. The rest, be it massacre at marriage party and torture in Ashaniketan, were transitory. Ganeshan switched off the TV and poured out some more tea. Naseema joined him at the table.

She said there was tension in the city. An incident like that could easily detonate a communal riot. Especially when the terrorists were of one particular religious group. Two bomb blasts had taken place recently in close interval. Thirty people had been killed. Fear and anger were building up. People were avoiding crowded places. Shops were pulling down shutters as soon as dusk fell. Streets looked deserted in the evenings. Ganeshan pointed out that it was the job of media to sensationalise everything and much of what they report is usually overblown.

Ganeshan was not meeting any of his friends lately. When he felt he needed human presence, he would go out to a park or an ancient monument and sit on a bench and read. Naseema was leaving home early and coming back before evening. She said that Vasundhara had visited the Saathi office once but didn't stay too long since she was feeling unwell. Her present complaint was that she heard her own voice while talking.

Ganeshan remembered one of Aman's poems:

When you are talking but your mind wanders
When you are speaking a lie,
When your words are inconsequential,
You begin hearing your own voice.
That voice you have not noticed till then,
That voice you nevertheless recognise as yours.

Since reading it, Ganeshan wondered how and under what circumstances Aman must have experienced such a thing. Vasundhara might have different reasons for hearing her own voice. Perceptions change from individual to individual and answers would not be forthcoming from either quarter now. What we call 'wonder' is one filled with light, a welcoming or exciting feeling. One must not peer into the abyss of darkness it holds behind the light.

He looked down at the newspaper he had been holding while lost in thought. The centre page was a full-page advertisement of a tutorial institute that coached students for various competitive examinations. The whole page was covered with stamp size photographs of children, arranged neatly in rows and columns. Children the school claimed to have coached have passed with top ranks in the recently held entrance examinations. Under each photograph was given the name of the boy or girl to prove the authenticity of the claim.

'Something is haunting you, Ganeshan,' said Naseema. 'Is it the massacre at the marriage party? Keep your mind steady and clear of disturbing influences, Ganeshan. That will give it strength.'

'Naseema, I was looking at these heads, I mean faces.' He turned the leaf of the paper towards her.

'They would have displayed the photographs of those twenty-five persons like this, too, had they been able to lay their hands on them,' Naseema said wryly.

'They would have. But I am not exactly thinking of that now.'

Naseema looked at him questioningly.

'See, there are about two hundred children on this one page,' Ganeshan went on. 'Enough children to form one small school. If they were not children, it could have constituted a small village. But this is not the photo of a crowd nor of an assembly or procession. All of them are marked separately and individually. Each head has been cut and fixed in a rectangle and arranged in rows and columns. Everyone has been made to stand alone, as an individual. Each has been given a name and address. For example, this boy's name is Naresh Kumar Oberoi. His body has been cut and removed from him. His hands, legs, heart and kidney. As if Naresh Kumar Oberoi is only a face. That alone constitutes his identity. We don't know whether the boy is disabled or dwarfed—'

Ganeshan stopped abruptly. He in fact wanted to say something else. What guarantee was there that those faces were actually of people whose names were written below? What if above Naresh Kumar's name was Vijay Menon's photograph? Above Vijay Menon's was one of Mohammad Shukur's, or Peter Desouza's? He withdrew his forefinger from Naresh Kumar's face.

Naseema sat with a smile of amusement on her lips and a coffee cup in hand, listening to Ganeshan's diatribe. The peace brought to her face by spirituality disturbed him.

'Well,' Naseema stood up and said, 'Everyone does not look at people like that. This is the month of our annual medical checkup. I have taken an appointment. At least the clinic people don't think of us as mere faces. We are, to them, our blood parameters and our organs. As we age, we become heart, kidney, brain, gall bladder and prostate.'

Ganeshan joined in the laughter.

THIRTY-FIVE

The building had three floors above ground and a basement. All were occupied by the clinic. One had to start in the basement, with registration, payment and other formalities. Two girls sitting there would provide you with a small book, which became your passport and a road map to proceed with your journey. Once you were done at the counter, the traveller in you would gradually withdraw and you became a travelling object. For some time, of course, you would try to believe that you were contributing something by asking where to go, whom to meet etc., but soon that arrogance would vanish. The realisation would soon dawn on you that you are no longer under your own control. Even receiving instructions and complying with them would happen so mechanically that you wouldn't notice.

The tests were many. Some to be done before food, some after, some with medicines injected, some just exercises. All were routine ones, as both Ganeshan and Naseema were healthy and without any problems or deficiencies. Viewing others sitting around and complaining and narrating their pains, they felt a little awkward to be in such a place with healthy and fit bodies.

Although they were initially separated and made to go different ways, they again met in corridors meant for waiting, only to separate again. At one such junction, they stumbled upon Colonel Desouza.

'Colonel, you always say we should be in our control,' Ganeshan made a friendly dig. 'Here we are reduced to just bodies with no propellants or controls.'

'I used to add one more sentence before that,' the colonel said, laughing. 'That things are not in our control. Your freedom to decide if you want to be a body or soul is taken away when you are in a hospital. Even when you have no ailments, like in your case.'

It stung, what he said. Desouza, unlike the two of them, was not there on their annual pilgrimage to validate their good health. Clinics were part of his daily life; he had many ailments, some pretty serious ones though you would never find him complaining about them.

Just then, someone emerged from a lab, the doctor of their colony. The doctor was always flippant about health, his and everyone else's.

'See the irony,' came his remark immediately. 'People who come seeking treatment are exactly the ones who have to take care of the health of the public and protect them from enemies!'

'Because they are in the know of ailments. The people are not!' was Ganeshan's rejoinder.

'That is also true,' acknowledged the doctor. 'In fact, people's ailments are still without medicines.'

'What disease has fallen upon all of you?' asked Naseema.

'Disease has fallen upon everyone, Naseema madam,' the colonel said in an attempt to change the topic. 'For us, who go out every morning and return home in the same shape in the evening, it is mere chance. We could be waylaid, attacked or bombed any moment outside. Sometimes you are targeted for yourself, at others you are mistaken for someone else.'

'Instead of the few hours from morning to evening, if you consider a longer period, it might appear that the disease is entirely different,' the doctor added. 'Colonel saheb, the chance you mentioned plays out in other ways, too. For example, what is the meaning of these names we proudly grant ourselves like doctor, soldier, government employee, journalist and trader? It is mere chance. We could very well have been a ragpicker, pickpocket, criminal, terrorist. All have the same limbs and organs. Hands, legs, heart, kidney...'

'Why are you talking like this, doctor saheb?' the colonel asked, placing his hand on his back.

'I have not yet been able to come to terms with what I heard in the morning news,' the doctor said. 'Do you know who was that terrorist who fell from the bike and was killed by his accomplices? The police have identified him as Shamsher, an intellectual and artist well known in our social circles.'

Naseema and Ganeshan were stunned. He found a bench for Naseema to sit and brought a bottle of water from the counter at the corner of the corridor. It was too much for her to bear.

The doctor's name was called out, and he left for the test. Desouza apparently didn't remember Shamsher whom he had met at Ganeshan's house, and Ganeshan didn't want to remind him. Desouza himself wanted to take the conversation in a different direction and started talking about the school where he worked. He again invited him to visit the place.

'Come this week itself, if possible,' he insisted. 'The sponsor of the school is a very interesting person. His name is Swami. The whole week he would be at the school. It is in his farmhouse, you know. You will not forget him if you meet him.'

Desouza also was called in, and Ganeshan and Naseema were left alone.

'How will Vasundhara take this, I am worried,' said Naseema. 'She lived with him for over a year.'

Ganeshan sat by her side and took her hand in his. 'Who knows if that was not the reason for their parting,' he said. 'And for her present state...'

THIRTY-SIX

'Do you not think it improper to represent a person with a photo that only shows their face?'

Ganeshan was taken aback with that question, as if he heard his own voice.

There was a dry smile on Suchitra Behan's face when she asked it. It looked like a dry leaf that had flown in from somewhere and was resting on her lips, shaking.

Suchitra Behan was the head of Pratiksha Bhavan, a special kind of school where colonel Desouza was doing voluntary work. A middle-aged woman with a thin frame, a yellow sari wrapped carelessly around her. Suchitra and her husband Anup belonged to a voluntary organisation involved in developmental activities in the northeast areas, helping villagers stand on their own feet. One morning, a few people from a militant outfit styled as the Liberation Army came to their camp, saying they wanted to know about the work they were doing. They took Anup with them to apparenly visit the site.

He didn't return. The search to locate him went on for months but didn't yield any result. Then they got a message from the militants, that Anup would be released if his organisation packs up and leaves the place. Reluctantly, they wound up. But Anup did not return. Instead a newspaper report appeared saying Anup had slipped and fallen in a gorge while trying to escape the militants. He could not be traced after that. The police thought that they must have killed him on the very same day of kidnapping. Defeated, the organisation shifted their work elsewhere. Some of them still hoped that Anup would return one day and join them. This school was Suchitra's idea. In the industrialist–philanthropist Swami, she met a like-minded person. He allotted a portion of his twenty-five acre farm in the outskirts of the city to the school without any hesitation. He also constructed the buildings they needed for the work.

In fact, the school formed an integral part of the farm, occupying a portion marked with hillocks and beautiful rock outcrops. On one hill was a place of worship that did not belong to any particular religion. On others stood the settlement and hostels. The school, playgrounds and garden were below, on the plains. Ganeshan found that the children spent more time in play, doing handicrafts and in prayers than in formal classes.

The dry leaf smile flew away from Suchitra Behan's lips.

'Do you see those two boys sitting there chatting under the tree?' she said drawing Ganeshan's attention to them. 'The elder one is who feels so. His father was a granthi in a gurudwara. One evening, as father and son were closing up the shrine, two men arrived on a motorcycle. Everyone had left by then. But the boy saw everything. They had struck his father down and with a sword cut off his head. They picked up the head and drove away holding it by his long hair. For a long time, the boy was alone with the headless body of his father. Till the village woke up and people gathered. There were religious objections in cremating a body without the head. As for the boy, he cannot bear seeing headshots anymore. He would fly into a rage and tear it up like a mad boy. Here we are very careful about that. We cannot imagine the havoc violence plays on our minds.'

'Perhaps the violent history of humanity is behind the practice of representing a person with their face,' mused Ganeshan.

The dry leaf smile reappeared. 'This boy has taught us the need to see a human being as a whole. It has become a part of our education system here.'

'There is a girl of twelve years here, she cannot sleep during the night,' Suchitra Behan continued to tell another child's story. 'She sleeps only during the daytime. Five months back, four or five people broke down the doors to her house in the middle of the night and shot dead her policeman father, mother, grandmother, a younger sister and a baby brother. Through the night, she keeps asking the same question: why did they spare her? That question is very relevant. They left the poor girl alive intentionally. It is not sufficient to kill, but the act has to be preserved like a video recording. What better recording than the mind of an innocent witness? You know fear and hate are seeds that do not need any water or fertiliser to grow. 'Do you object to my comparing them with plants?' she asked almost as a challenge.

Ganeshan said nothing.

A boy came to her with a worn-out wheel bearing in his hand. Patting his back, she asked him to say namaste to Ganeshan.

The boy did so.

'We have a small machine shop here,' she said. 'We collect worn out machine parts from workshops. The children make various devices out of them according to their imagination. Kanwal is always there. He wants to become a mechanic. He likes machines very much.'

'No,' the boy emphatically denied what she said, throwing away the machine part. 'I want to become a policeman. I want to hunt down the men who killed my father and finish them off.'

Suchitra Behan's face fell.

Ganeshan tried to reason with the boy. 'Son, the job of policemen is not killing or taking revenge. They are only to implement the law.'

'But I want to kill them. If I get my hands on them, I won't arrest them, I will shoot them.'

When he went away, Suchitra picked up the machine part from the ground and said as if to herself. 'Perhaps in the company of the other children, he will change.'

Children of men killed by policemen usually have no opportunity of witnessing the act. They only see the bodies when it reaches their home. Some say their fathers were militants, some otherwise. They have no idea what a militant meant. Still, they want to become militants when they grow up.

Desouza came to take him to Swami. Beyond the hills, the farm and farmhouse were on relatively level ground. They walked towards it.

THIRTY-SEVEN

Swami was really an interesting personality. Rich, honest and gentle, Ganeshan found no reason to doubt these adjectives given to him by Desouza. Swami had plenty of business interests but he was not paying much attention to them these days, it was told.

Desouza left after introducing Ganeshan to Swami. Swami was in the vermiculture section talking to a customer. Finishing that, he accompanied him.

A portion of the farm was allotted to experimental farming of rare and special items. Then there were grapes, mushrooms, flowers, pineapples, herbs and such. He also had cattle, goats, fowls and a section for the production of organic manure. They did not use pesticides or chemical fertilisers in the farm.

He talked to Ganeshan as he walked about checking in with people at each stop. He looked a bit reticent in the beginning but opened up eventually. Desouza had told him about Ganeshan it seemed, but Ganeshan knew nothing about

Swami except the bare minimum. Swami was not averse to filling him in. Ganeshan was not in the habit of talking about personal matters to others, but he did not consider the world unfolding before him through Ashaniketan, Cawasji and the dhaba manager personal. Swami listened as Ganeshan told him the story.

'I am also looking for someone,' he said. 'But I don't know where and when I would meet him.' After a while he became reflective, 'I did not think I was quite this overweight,' he panted as they talked while walking. He continued, 'And even if I manage to meet him, it may not prove to be useful.'

Swami did not continue and instead led him to the shed where mushrooms were being cultivated. Workers were collecting umbrellas of mushrooms, which had freshly come out on the beds of straw. It was comfortable in shade, cool and moist, coming in from the sun. But Swami didn't stay there long and returned to the sun and dust outside which he seemed to like more.

'Ganeshan, I am alone today,' said Swami. 'The only companion I had was my wife Kausalya. For her, too, I was the only one.'

Swami and Kausalya had no children. While Swami drowned himself in the business, she embraced farming. It was for her he purchased and started the farm. She hailed from an old farming family in the foothills. He knew virtually nothing about agriculture. His was a business family, and he wanted to grow what he inherited from his father. But unfortunately, both their family lines would end with them. After buying the farm, which Kausalya wanted, they shifted from the bungalow in the city to the farmhouse. He certainly liked the calm evenings, but he was happy with whatever made Kausalya happy. They loved each other so much.

'Kausalya took ill all of a sudden. What started as small ailments was finally diagnosed as total failure of both the kidneys. Doctors found my kidneys totally unfit. We had to look for a donor.'

Swami sat on a platform built under a huge neem tree. The way he sat with his hands on his knees, and cheeks sagging, made him suddenly look very old. But Swami was actually much younger. Sorrow had taken its toll.

'It was then that I came to know the intricacies and intrigues involved in kidney donation,' Swami continued. 'Middlemen ruled and dealings were murky and underhand. The agent I got was from a town in down south. He would bring the donor only three days before the operation. The agent was to be known as agent, the donor as donor. They would have no names. When the donor reached the city, the agent would put them up in a hotel. It was prohibited for me to see them or talk to them. I met the man only at the time of the formalities in the hospital. A boy in early twenties. He could have been my son.

It was obvious that he was very poor, and he was in dire need of money. He was afraid of looking at me. He kept his eyes on the agent who was always present between us. My wife wanted to know his name, in order to pray for him. We found it in his papers: Javed. It was then that the trouble started.'

Swami paused. Ganeshan didn't want to press him and waited.

Swami continued, 'Kausalya was a product of old traditions. A blind adherent to religion with all its prejudices and practices. A superstitious woman I would say. She must not know that her donor was a Muslim; she would refuse to go through the operation, even if it killed her. I reluctantly put the problem before the agent. Without a moment's hesitation he changed the name of the boy to Jaidev and showed the papers to me carefully hiding the address part of it. I knew it would be false even if I saw it. I saw Javed being taken out on the trolley after the operation. When I heard him calling Allah the Merciful in his semi-conscious state, I was shattered. How mean and cruel I had been. I had used that poor boy in such an undignified way. I took away his religion, God and individuality, and he was giving life to my wife. I could not forgive myself. For some time, to be frank, he was more on my mind than my wife. Everything was wrong, it was a sin that I had committed. But the deed was done. There was only one way to do penance, only one way that I had power to do, that was to compensate him financially for his priceless gift. But the trolley and Javed as well as the agent had already vanished and I could not find them again.'

For Swami, Javed's story did not end there. The agent had so easily changed the name from Javed into Jaidev. How could he even be sure that Javed was Javed? People often give false identities in such transactions. The address in hospital records also proved to be non-existent. All he knew was that Javed was from the south, but was even that true? The doctors only knew him as a body. They extracted a kidney from it. Javed disappeared but left that kidney with Kausalya. But that, too, didn't last. Her body rejected the transplant, and she died within a few months. Along with her, Javed's kidney, too, was burnt to ashes. Swami slowly retired to the farmhouse. He donated a portion of it to Suchitra Behan, and it became the Pratiksha Bhavan. In a few months, he too underwent a metamorphosis: the shrewd businessman became a dedicated and highly involved farmer.

'Do you feel close to Kausalya Devi now that you are a farmer? Is that how you identify yourself now?' Ganeshan asked.

Swami took out a photo from his wallet and looked at it.

'What is identity? What is the picture that an individual evokes in your mind?' Swami asked. 'Isn't it the special characteristics of a person? It could be the really fine particulars of their behaviour. Some quirk in their personality. It does not have to be their name, their address or their photo, does it? It could even be just an organ, a kidney for instance. In fact, when you think about it, a person's identity may not have anything to do with them at all. They may just be like a springboard to launch an exploration of discovery. A symbol to start from, which can lead to a whole wide canvas of experiences.'

Ganeshan listened bemused. It appears he was to be haunted by photos, faces and identities, no matter where he went.

'Is that the photo of Kausalya Devi that you have there?'

Swami shook his head. 'This is Javed's photo.'

'So now instead of Kausalya Devi's photo he is carrying Javed's!' Ganeshan thought to himself. But instead he asked, 'How did you get it?'

Swami still didn't offer to show him the photo. Instead, he continued with his story. 'I had gone to the south for business. I took an evening off and went for a stroll through the streets of the town. To my surprise, I bumped into Javed there! He was working as a taxi driver. When I called out his name, he did not respond; who knows if that was even his name. But I called again and eventually he did. This time there was no fear on his face, only a deep sadness. He didn't talk much. But I learned that just as the story of the kidney was a failure on my side, so it was on Javed's side. Javed had sold his kidney for money to get his sister married. That marriage was a failure. Her husband had another wife. Their squabbles ended in her death. He pushed her out of a moving train and killed her. Javed had lost his kidney as well as his sister. When I heard his story, I decided to bring him here with me.'

Swami wanted him to live with him, not as an employee but as a son. This time he himself asked him to change his religion but for another reason. He wanted to adopt him as a son but could not do that as Islamic law did not permit adoption. But Javed left the lure of a fortune and disappeared.

Swami sat down shaking his head.

'Why did you take that route? You could have passed on your wealth to him with a will, there was no need to adopt…'

Swami had a sad smile on his face. 'If Kausalya had lived, Javed would have lived in her body. God didn't wish it that way. I thought by adopting him as my son I would be able to repay his debt. Passing over my wealth felt like an insult to his service, like a payment, I wanted it to be more than that. I didn't realise that religion was such a big part of a man's identity. I wronged him again. When I made the proposal he did not say anything for two days. But on the third day, he was gone. I have to find him again, Ganeshan. If he can't be my son, let it be so. Let him be Javed, or whoever he wants to be.'

'We shall find him,' Ganeshan said impulsively.

'How?' Swami's eyes brightened.

And Ganeshan wondered what prompted him to make such a commitment. The only Javed he had known was a man who used to be Cawasji's driver.

'Please show me the photograph,' said Ganeshan.

Swami showed him the photo readily.

But it was just a photo, a headshot of an unremarkable-looking young man. Ganeshan did not remember the face of Cawasji's driver even though he wanted to compare the two. Why he thought they would be the same, he couldn't tell.

'Didn't you discover him in a distant town on a crowded street?' said Ganeshan lamely.

'It is a small world.'

THIRTY-EIGHT

'Cawasji.'

'Ganeshan, I was expecting your call. Have you got them?'

'Whom?'

'Then they must be on their way. They will reach you soon, some more children.'

'You mean...'

'Yes, I have freed some more children from the register. I think it is time to start on the staff now. Guards and the workers, cooks, warders...We have already brought down a good portion of Ashaniketan...Why are you silent Ganeshan? Do you still think this institution deserves to exist?'

'No, but institutions are—'

'All have degenerated. They all have turned into brothels or child abuse centres.'

'Cawasji, institutions—'

'Ganeshan, it is not earthquakes that kill but buildings. Not wars but soldiers that carry out destruction.'

'Cawasji, institutions are products of civilisation.'

'Will it not be more correct to say that creating institutions is a process of civilisation?'

'That, too, may be correct. But what I mean is that it is not buildings but badly built buildings that kill.'

'You maybe right. But we cannot wait for earthquakes to identify poorly built structures.'

'You are an architect, Cawasji.'

'Every scientist is now questioning his own science, denying it or reconstructing it.'

'This is anarchy, Cawasji.'

'Anarchy comes later. What happens now is collapse. Collapse of all that has been raised.'

'I have heard that the most important appliance for an architect is mortar. Bond…leave that. I called to ask you about that driver Javed, is he still with you?'

'Why, do you know him?'

'I don't know him, but I want to know about him. How does he look?'

'Difficult to say. I am bad with remembering appearances, I can't even tell if a man I knew had a moustache or not. Anyway, you have to give up on this quest. Two months ago he left me without any warning. He did not even collect his last month's salary.'

'Oh! You don't know where he has gone?'

'Why should we know, Ganeshan? Why should we stand in the way of people's freedom?'

'Cawasji…'

'Sorry, but I feel you shouldn't strain your mind like this.'

'Do you know anything concerning this man?'

'Uhm. I think he had acquired some new friends recently. I wondered if they were Pappan's men, or for that matter, Kaku's. But this was just a suspicion, nothing more than that. You already know something about Pappan, maybe about Kaku, too?'

'What I have read in magazines.'

'Don't you think there is more drama in Kaku's story?'

'The papers seem to say so. So, Javed's friends…'

'Ganeshan, this is just a suspicion, I have no basis for it. Perhaps they were good friends of his. New people coming to town from villages, carrying the burden of losses. Picking up new drama here.'

'What kind of losses?'

'Ganeshan, you are the one who counts every fissure as a loss, every transplanting an uprooting.'

'Yes, but so is every trowel of mortar a gain.'

As he replaced the receiver, the doorbell rang. Cawasji's courier had arrived.

For a while, Ganeshan didn't feel like doing anything. He just sat looking at the rain-washed plants and lush green grass growing in the front garden. Then he opened the packet. This time there were five pages. Five children liberated and dispatched to him by Cawasji. As if they were now his responsibility.

Perhaps Cawasji's desire to liberate the children imprisoned in the torture chamber that was Ashaniketan was more intense than Ganeshan's. Ganeshan couldn't understand the methods or mechanism he planned for the purpose. At the same time, Ganeshan knew that for Cawasji, children meant only some pages of the register. Whether the boys there were called Vijay, Shankar or Gopal was not of any interest to Cawasji. In fact, it was beyond his understanding. Names, pictures, height, weight, age—all such matters he passed over to Ganeshan. Once removed from the situation, he was not interested in the pages. Just as he was not even ready to recall the face of his driver who had been with him for such a long time.

Ganeshan spread all the pages he had received from Cawasji so far on his table. The pages were obviously not in any order. Even the last lot sent to him was not continuous. Gaps everywhere. Between the groups and within a group. From each page through the rectangle of a photo, like through a window, the face of one child stared at him. The other side of the window was sometimes well lit, at other times dim and sometimes totally dark. The background, like the faces, was faded as the photos were old and poorly kept. Who can imagine what the world of each of those children lying beyond the window frame was? Ganeshan could not, perhaps no one could. Perhaps even the children might not like to revisit places from where they had torn themselves away. Aman puts all the blame on the walls. Walls bear windows and make one conscious of the world lying beyond windows, showing some and darkening others. In the end, what remains are windows. Sometimes not even windows, just the geometry of a rectangle.

Ganeshan got up from the chair to take out from his files of cuttings a photo that had appeared in the newspapers some time back. It was not an easy task. Initially, he used to file the cuttings according to dates. Then, at some point, he orgnised them subject-wise. Cuttings and newspapers, reports and photos—all got mixed up. He remembered neither the date on which the photo appeared nor the time when he switched over to the new system. He went through half a dozen fat files like a traveller through a map who didn't know the route. At last, his perseverance was rewarded.

It was a photo from an old socialist country presently torn by ethnic and communal violence. Four little boys playing soldier. They were crouching behind a wall of sandbags. One of them had a toy gun pointed to the sky while another sat on his haunches. Others, too, looked in the same direction.

The postures and gestures were typically adult, while the faces were beatifically innocent.

He took it and kept it along with the Cawasji collection. He didn't know why.

THIRTY-NINE

It was after another great hunt that Ganeshan unearthed the story of Kaku Supplier, the head of Kaku gang, from his files. He had collected it in his folder of newspaper cuttings; he had come across the piece among cuttings that used to be circulated daily at office. Scrutinising the media reports related to city affairs was a routine duty for him. But this one stuck in his mind, maybe due to its macabre details. So he had kept it.

Nand Kishore who came to be known as Kaku in later years was one of the several thousand children orphaned in the Great Partition riots, and he washed into the city as part of the flood of refugees. Kishore started his life as a servant doing cleaning and washing jobs at a roadside eatery. When his master moved to the town looking for better pastures and started a food catering establishment that went by the name of The Tent House, he, too, became part of it. The Tent House did the complete work of erecting shamianas, providing furniture and preparing and serving food for parties.

Once his master was arranging a party in the bungalow of a minister. Kishore was in the kitchen, set up in the spacious compound at the back of the bungalow. He had gone to a corner covered by trees to dump the waste when something bizarre happened. He stumbled upon something in the darkness of the evening and realised that it was a human hand projecting out of freshly dug earth. He stifled a cry and ran to his master to report it. What he got was a slap on his face, which was his master's habitual reaction to those who talked about things not related to their work. But then he accompanied the boy to the site with a torch. Together they examined the projecting hand and found that it was that of a woman, with bangles. Obviously, the result of an imperfect and hurried burial. It seemed to be calling out for help like a raised hand of a woman drowning. The two of them, however, decided not to offer any help. Instead, they decided to complete what her tormenters had left unfinished. They covered the hand with branches and leaves they collected from the surroundings. Then the master placed his hand on the shoulder of the boy like a father and advised him, 'We have come here with a contract for the minister's party. That is our only concern here. You haven't seen anything here, and you don't know anything.' Someone else's crime bonded them together.

But they had not been unobserved in their attempt to complete the burial. Late in the night, when the party was over, the master was summoned to the minister's chamber.

What transpired there Kishore didn't know. But after the incident, the boy became his master's confidant and right-hand man. The contractor's business grew and prospered, perhaps the minister had something to do with it, who knows. Kishore rose to become a partner. Kishore learnt an important lesson: hands sticking out of the grounds are a good thing. If you keep them quiet, your own hands grow stronger.

Later, Kishore started his own catering service. He came to be known as Kaku Supplier; he rather liked it. Now Kaku owned a number of hotels in the city from ordinary to posh types. His large farmhouse outside the city limits has a posh open-air restaurant in beautiful natural settings which has become one of the most sought after meeting places for the city elite. Every Saturday evening, important personalities in fashion, art and media world could be seen there. But the man called Nand Kishore would not be among them. He remained the supplier and in the background, more at home with middlemen, agents, pimps and professional killers. Though their activities did not really overlap, Pappan and Kaku were always at loggerheads, and their gangs openly fought.

Ganeshan finished reading the article and went to bed. In the morning, however, he went through it once more over a cup of tea. Naseema walked in and saw him at the coffee table. Pointing to the loft above the door, she said, 'Ganeshan, I need you to take down that green bag we have there.'

'Wouldn't it be better to take a suitcase?' he suggested.

Naseema shook her head. 'That would be too big, I don't have that many things to carry.'

'The suitcase brings a business look, doesn't it?'

Naseema chuckled. She was going away for a camp organised by the ashram. A meditation camp, in the mountains. She did say the name of the place, but it didn't register in Ganeshan's mind. A place blessed with extreme natural beauty and spiritual atmosphere, she said. Then, there was also the attraction of cool climate since the weather in the city had turned most oppressive. Ganeshan told her to carry sufficient warm clothing as the sudden change in weather could cause illness.

Ganeshan picked up the stool and took out the bag Naseema wanted from the loft. He dusted and cleaned it. Naseema immediately transferred her belongings to it from the suitcase in which they were kept previously.

She was just finishing up when Rishi walked in unannounced; they were both surprised and a little apprehensive.

'Everything ok, Rishi? Any news from Seeta?' asked Naseema.

'No news, madam,' Rishi shook his head. 'I enquired in every publishing house I could think of, and she is not working with any of them.'

'Whatever has happened to this girl,' Naseema wondered aloud. 'Such a bright girl. Very loving, too. I will also do some search from my end. But it will have to wait till I come back.'

Ganeshan told Rishi that Naseema was going out on a meditation camp arranged by her ashram.

'Oh,' Rishi was visibly disappointed. 'How long will it be?'

'Two weeks,' she said. 'May be extended by a day or two.'

They sat around the coffee table. Naseema prepared a light coffee for Rishi as he wanted it without sugar. As they talked, the ashram van arrived. Naseema bid them bye and got into it.

When the van took off, Rishi said, 'I came to tell you about another girl, Ganeshan.'

Ganeshan looked at him questioningly.

'I didn't know of Naseema's trip,' Rishi said. 'It would have been of interest to both of you.'

'Tell me, Rishi. I shall convey it to her.'

'Zoya is her name. She stepped into my home suddenly yesterday without any kind of prior indication. A girl in her twenties, pleasant and likeable. A research worker or freelance journalist or something, she said. It appeared there was no special reason behind her visit. I asked how she knew of me, and she replied with a smile: are we not of the same tribe? We talked about nothing in particular. She told me she has read my pieces in the newspapers, and that she writes poems sometimes. It was kind of awkward, and I was feeling a bit lost. Then, suddenly she said she knew Aman, and that they were old friends. I think that is what she actually came to tell me.'

'What did she say?' Ganeshan bent forward eagerly. 'She should have come to us.'

'Calm down Ganeshan, she will,' Rishi said. 'She didn't say much. If I can piece together what she said, it was something like this: For such a young age, the task Aman undertook, that is to create an experience of human presence among people, was not an easy one, especially in a world more and more fractured by fissures or absences, where a new crack seems to appear every passing day. I am trying to repeat the exact words she used the way she used them. I asked her if the expression of young age didn't apply to her also. "Isn't it true that such tasks can only be accomplished by young ones?" She just laughed, then became serious. Without answering my question, she said, "One day I want to go and meet his parents, I want to talk to them." I saw her eyes glistening with unshed tears when she said this. Then she abruptly got up and left. I felt that her visit to me was a preparation for visiting you. Anyway, I thought I should come here and tell you both.'

'Thank you, Rishi, thank you very much.' Ganeshan touched Rishi's hand resting on the table. 'Her phone number, address, anything?'

'She left nothing,' Rishi shook his head. 'We only have her name. She said she would be meeting you soon. I didn't press.'

'I don't know if I came at an inappropriate time. When I saw Naseema now, I began to wonder how she would take it.'

Ganeshan was silent for some time. Then he said, 'Naseema is on the path of spirituality. She has found peace in that, it appears. To that extent, it is good. Returning to something she has successfully managed to forget…I don't know whether that would be good for her. Sometimes I am unable to understand the way her mind works. Come Rishi, I want to show you something.'

Ganeshan led Rishi to the garden at the back of their house. The bougainvillea had grown further. Its branches were hanging further down. Ganeshan had not tried to touch it since Naseema stopped him. Raising the branches, he showed Rishi the cane basket underneath. The basket was half-eaten away by white ants and the round stones of varying colours were still inside.'

'Do these stones tell you something?' Ganeshan asked him.

Rishi took some of them in his hand and said reflecting, 'Nomadic people collect such stones in baskets and carry them with them. They regard them as gods. A basket full of gods. For each group, one basket. How did this come here?'

'I don't know,' Ganeshan shook his head. 'Naseema prohibited me from touching them. Not just prohibited, she got very agitated that day.'

Rishi laughed, 'Then it must be the same thing. She must have acquired them from somewhere.'

'But why should one fear them, especially if they are gods?'

Rishi shrugged his shoulders. 'One nomadic group once told me that their gods were stolen away by another group! It was interesting. Proselytisers and missionaries worry about believers being stolen away from gods. Here we have gods being stolen away from believers! What a coincidence, I just completed an article on this subject and sent it off to the paper.'

'Naseema was not prepared to talk about it,' said Ganeshan. 'So I didn't ask anything further. When I come to think of it, once before also she had prevented me from cutting the branches of this bougainvillea. She perhaps wanted them to hide the stones. Maybe she dislikes these gods.'

'These must have come here via Saathi. I shall find out from them.'

'Rishi, you know that I don't like to go behind Naseema's back.'

'It is not that, Ganeshan. Don't take it that way. Stolen gods are a part of my research subject and whatever I do would be in that context.'

Ganeshan seated Rishi in the drawing room and went upstairs to Aman's room and came back with a sheet of paper.

'Let your article on stolen gods come out. I look forward to reading it,' he said. 'Now, read this poem. This is Aman's poem. Yesterday Cawasji said something to me about his missing driver. What he said prompted me to dig up reports about the Kaku gang in the newspapers that I had filed away some time back. The whole evening I was busy with that. How difficult it is to find something from the old papers! We know that it is there but can't find it. The search sometimes takes you along some other road and finally you end up at something else. This is perhaps life, the character of it. If we accept it to be so, perhaps we would be able to face even the most tragic situations with composure. Starvation deaths, bomb blasts, mindless massacres…what do you say? Aman's poem somehow came to my mind as we talked.'

Rishi read Aman's poem:

Do we truly see the world before us?
Who sees it in its true form? Is it children?
Is it the thieves, the policemen?
The old story of the blind men and the elephant
Where each sees a different part
Is no longer valid.
Everyone sees the world in full,
Or turns what he sees into the whole,

Keeping the eyes tightly open,
Or, as they say, widely shut.
That is the new way.
Each one working with the whole world
In his hands.
Everyone is carrying in his hand death,
Death of his friends, foes and everyone,
Like a grenade.

Ganeshan poured some more coffee into their cups, and they silently sipped from them. The sun had turned the outer world into a vast furnace. Humidity inside made the ceiling fans ineffective.

'Now I feel I didn't come at an inappropriate time,' said Rishi, idly massaging the knee of his shorter leg. 'In fact, I knew virtually nothing of Aman. I had just seen him a few times, that was all.'

'I too have that feeling sometimes.'

'You once told me that you could not become close with him, after his return.'

'And, imagine, this was when he was a present, filling the fissures created by his absence.'

'When did this thought come to you?'

'One can't really say exactly when one understands something, Rishi. And mind you, to understand a thing, its presence is not essential.'

'What was the other thing you wanted to tell me?'

'You should forgive me, Rishi, it might be just my anxious mind overthinking. You told me that the organisation where Seeta worked was owned by Pappan and that she had some problems there. I only pray no one harms her.'

'Ganeshan, whenever this fear rises in my mind, someone calls me up and tells me that they got a call from her. Even yesterday, I got a call. She is not giving her contact number to anyone, but I think she is not in danger.'

FORTY

Fear had become a mainstay on the citizen's plate, with ample helpings served by newspapers. Fear, like salt, is an ingredient in all recipes. Fear written on the faces of those waiting for the school bus in the morning; fear in the calls of hawkers, in the silence of the passers-by. Shutters come down on the shops by evening, roads become empty after dusk. The family crowds around the TV for the nine o'clock news to find out the balance sheet of the day. What they find is fear embellished with more fear.

Ganeshan felt detached, the kind of detachment he hadn't felt for a while now. The day lay before him without any promise. The sky was overcast, and it was drizzling on and off. These were perhaps the last rains of the season. It was time for monsoon to withdraw. Then the air would grow dry again, in preparation of winter. Ganeshan sat on the steps of the veranda watching the rain and the play of the sun and clouds. A cool breeze waltzed with the raindrops.

The younger neighbours were getting ready to go to their workplace. Children had already boarded the school buses, and housewives were busy with daily chores. There were a few like him surveying the rain from the veranda steps. He had a complete view of the colony from his vantage point. The rain suddenly gathered momentum into a heavy downpour, which drew a curtain between him and the rest, isolating him totally. He went in and got a cup of tea to go with the performance outside and again settled himself on the veranda.

When was Naseema supposed to reach the ashram? He felt guilty about not asking. She had said she was going, and he had only said okay. She had been so excited about the trip, and would not have noticed his lack of response. He decided that when she gets back he would tell her about Zoya and also about Aman's poems.

The rain transformed into a hail. Soon there was a white carpet over the grass and a minor flood in the road. Tomorrow's papers would now be all set with shots of the hailstones and cars and people wading through the waters.

The rain kept Ganeshan closeted in the house till noon. The afternoon sun broke through the clouds once the rains subsided. It painted yellow a house here or a bunch of trees there or a patch of lawn yonder. The cool breeze and the pleasant sun invited Ganeshan outside.

Ganeshan stopped his car in front of one of the largest parks of the city. He walked on the lawns, chasing the shadows cast by the clouds on the grass. The grass was washed clean, the ground was soft with moisture, and he took his shoes off to walk barefoot.

There again, to his surprise, he met inspector Tarun Kumar. This time it certainly felt like a chance encounter.

FORTY-ONE

A chance encounter, is it even possible in a pursuit? Should one even be trying to ascribe cause and effect to such encounters? Not just with inspector Tarun Kumar but with anyone for that matter. Perhaps chance encounters work to erase the trails of a chase. Is there a chase which does not culminate in an encounter? Which nomad has not discovered a refugee within themselves at some point of their journey? Has there been a refugee who has not wondered if the flight is older than them?

Tarun Kumar alternated between running and walking on the jogging track. Ganeshan was sitting on one of the benches lining it. He let the inspector pass once and decided to acknowledge him if he came around.

He came around the track again, and Ganeshan gave into fate and let his arm raise to flag him down. Tarun Kumar was in a white track suit. He appeared surprised. He stopped but continued to jog on the spot.

'Thank you, sir, for stopping me. I would have gone on like this and then fallen on the track eventually,' the inspector said, panting.

'You do really look like an unleashed animal, if you would excuse my saying so,' said Ganeshan jokingly.

'When a policeman is on leave, it is like being unleashed. At other times...'

'He breaks the rope,' completed Ganeshan.

'The difference may actually be whether there is a rope or not, I agree. In any case, I am on a three-day holiday. Relaxing...' he added gesturing towards himself, 'See, once you stop, you feel like sitting. I must sit for some time. If you don't mind, we can go to the park cafeteria and get something to drink.'

Ganeshan agreed. As he walked, the inspector's breathing slowed, and they found a table in the shade and called for some cold drinks.

'It was the festival of Ramnavami, and the fair was on in the mandir,' as soon as they settled down, Tarun Kumar began to narrate as if they had expressly come there for that purpose. 'Puja, bhajan and dance inside the mandir, while outside the crowd milled around in front of the shops selling sweets and little fancy wares. Lights and din of loudspeakers everywhere. Constable Chunni Ram on duty was looking for some place to rest his bottom, and he found it on a stone. Chunni Ram was a lazy fellow but very intelligent and clever. The conversation between two villagers standing nearby fell on his ears. They were narrating the heroic tales of two criminals of their village. The miscreants had met with unusual success after moving to the city, they said. The main character of the story had acquired great expertise in the art of kidnapping, which he had been practicing on a professional basis for bigwigs. But the fellow suddenly vanished after kidnapping two youngsters last year. This time he had not been lucky perhaps. It was believed that he must have been finished off by his victims. The storytellers were drunk, and Chunni Ram tactfully took them to the station on the charge of creating nuisance after drinking.'

'The intoxication of the two instantly evaporated at the station. Amazing things came out from the interrogation of the two. The kidnapper on hire in the story turned out to be one Mansoor whom the police had till then considered a small-time thief. The department had no knowledge that this man who started as a pickpocket had moved up in his trade and had started picking up whole persons. He had kidnapped two youngsters last year according to the village bards. He had enticed the duo, one of them a foreigner, to a trip saying that he would give them a rich experience of rural life of India. The militant organisation that had hired him for the job had promised a huge amount as fee. Can you imagine, sir, the modern management practices and contract systems of advanced capitalism have percolated down even to militant outfits!'

'Around the time mentioned by the villagers, four people had been reported as kidnapped in the city. Of them, two were together when they went missing, and the others were individual cases. The duo were youngsters, and one among them was a foreigner as stated by the villagers. It was widely believed that the kidnappers were militants as a foreign hostage was very valuable. But no militant outfits had claimed responsibility or raised a demand after the incident. It meant that the hostages had not fallen in the hands of the militants. Further probe revealed that around that time, Mansoor had been killed in an encounter according to the police records.'

Ganeshan grew impatient and asked, 'What about the hostages?'

Tarun Kumar said stoically, 'Nor have the hostages returned.'

Without giving Ganeshan the time to recover or ponder over the implications of that revelation, the inspector forged ahead, almost as if he was still running on the track. 'You must have heard on the news that one of the dead bodies left behind by the tragedy at the marriage reception had started breathing again,' he continued. 'It was Shamsher, a theatre artist and human rights activist, and one of the killers who was left behind to die. The man who was instrumental in making him come back to life is also an artist. You might know him, the painter and trade unionist, Koshi.'

'Koshi? What does he have to do with it?'

'I was right in presuming that you knew him. He has no formal training in art, yet he had been working as a part-time art instructor in some schools. Koshi had been the leader of the workers' union of a metal factory, which has been shut down. He also used to make an appearance as a tourist car driver-cum-guide. Koshi was the first to identify Shamsher. Apparently, they are neighbours. Koshi lost his wife and only daughter in the shooting. He had been in a state of shock for some time. He has not been able to reconcile the Shamsher he knew and the one he found there that day. He is now missing.'

Ganeshan could see the police officer's invisible finger pointing towards him. In the first story, he deliberately did not take Imtyaz's name. Here again, he didn't touch on the connection between Shamsher and Ganeshan. Instead, he had all the while been talking about Koshi. All said and done, one thing became clear: That both he and the officer were on the same track. Was one chasing the other or was this meeting indeed coincidental? The question has lost its relevance. It was as if the evening sun had emerged from the clouds just to throw its feeble light on that track, the track on which they found themselves together. And both Ganeshan as well as Tarun Kumar understood this.

'Who was the foreigner with Imtyaz, officer?' Ganeshan decided to come out and admit his knowledge.

'Christopher. Christopher was his name. An innocent enthusiast who came from Europe to India to study Indian classical dance forms. Like Imtyaz, Christopher, too, was deeply interested in the folk forms of music. They met in the city and had been together ever since. Imtyaz was a nobody, but he fell prey to the militants along with their real target, Christopher.'

'Hostages without a kidnapper to claim them.'

'Anybody can claim them. But they are still hostages. It is one of those cases that upset our reading.'

'Reading?'

'We, too, are readers, sir. The characters in our book are most often lifeless, victims. Like the twenty-five bodies spread out on the floor of the marriage pandal. Cutting them up and re-joining the pieces together, deconstructing and reconstructing, we work our way towards the authors. And here the author himself is dead and gone. And his hostages? They are playing hide and seek between the pages defying our search.'

'What do we know about Vijay, inspector? In which page, in how many pages, does he exist? Who is his creator?'

The inspector took a moment to answer, 'There is only one page there, sir. That small page on which he wrote your name.

The faint muted attempt of a poor nondescript character to become an author, which failed irretrievably.'

'Victims should remain victims, is that what you are saying inspector?'

'Who am I to say anything, sir? I am a poor policeman. He came to us as a body, dug up, partially decomposed. His appropriators had given him that fate. Dark mortuaries, autopsy tables, sample jars of viscera…'

'Yes, anyone with energy and soul and fire inside is reduced to a body when in the hands of a kidnapper.'

'You asked me about the pages of Vijay. A bizarre work it is, sir. Writers, too, are in a way kidnappers. A writer, however, fills a kidnapped man with whatever he wants and makes them extraordinary beings, unreal. A criminal, on the other hand, in one stroke empties all that makes him a man and leaves only a body. At the wedding reception, twenty-five of them including Koshi's wife and daughter turned into bodies in seconds. The kidnappers of Imtyaz and Christopher did not kidnap the persons, they were just bodies to them. Your pride in being Ganeshan is just like theirs, it will survive only till the day an author, a criminal arrives.'

'Where all can you look for a victim officer, a victim who has fallen out of the bag before was turned into a body?'

'If the kidnappers are militants, they can keep him in any dungeon as a hostage, till they realise their demands. If the victim has been taken away for brainwashing and recruitment into their gang, then we may expect him only in the state of a blown up fedayeen. Unlike those who join through faith, the militants don't trust the forcibly converted, they are only useful as weapons themselves. Then there are people taken away by occultist sects for sacrificial rituals. Those who are kidnapped for sexual abuse or drug trade would at some time surface as scum in the boiling cauldrons of society. Some of them may even be retrieved from the Ashaniketans and nariniketans. In nineteenth century Europe, ordinary people used to be caught from the streets and killed and sold as bodies to anatomy schools. Boys are also kidnapped for castration…whatever they are, they are bodies sir, mere bodies.'

What remained in the mind of Ganeshan at the end of inspector's monologue was the picture of a castrated body, not a dead one. A description he had read in a book years back, which left him almost insane. He had forcibly pushed it to the back of his mind to be stored away, but the inspector's words brought it all up like gastric reflux. A wooden stool with a penis-like projection strutting out in the middle of the room. The boy, kidnapped and brought to the secret den of the eunuchs is seated on the stool in such a way that the projection, well oiled, is fully inserted through his rectum, and the body is perfectly locked. He is dressed in red female attire and decked with flowers and garlands. A huge fire is kept burning in the fireplace in the front. The members of the society sing to the accompaniment of dhols and copper cymbals and dance around the fireplace. When the singing and dancing reach a crescendo, the operator eunuch, chewing pan, approaches him. He stands near the boy with an unconcerned air. Someone diverts the boy's attention to something and at that exact moment, with great dexterity, he flashes a knife and with one stroke completely cuts off the genitals of the boy—penis, testicles and all. The operator then spits the chewed paan spittle on the wound. Many boys die during this procedure. Some survive to live on as hijras.

FORTY-TWO

Ganeshan had come upon the book during Aman's disappearance. After reading it, he hid it at the bottom of a trunk so that Naseema wouldn't accidentally find it. The picture haunted him for several days. Even after burying it deep down in his mind, it sometimes bubbled up to the surface to torture him. Then Aman came back. And then came his death. A painless death perhaps with no time for him to realise he was dying. Somehow, that harrowing description stopped coming to his mind. Today, when the inspector brought it out again, he realised it has not lost any of its potency.

The fate of a victim being reduced to a mere body at the hands of a criminal might take different forms. The simplest and perhaps the kindest way might be the experience of Koshi's wife and daughter. At the other end of the spectrum, we have something like the one described in the book. An act like that did not end with slicing off of body parts. It changes you into another person, another gender, and you are condemned to live with that new identity for the rest of your life, a reminder of the violence done to you. When you yourself are the living proof of your annhilation.

What started as a dull, cloudy day that appeared to have nothing in store ended up like that. Back at home, Ganeshan pulled off his sweat-drenched clothes, went straight into the bathroom and stood under the shower for a long time. He wanted to wash off all the ugliness but to no avail. He switched on the TV. News blared out from every channel. The displaced prime minister of the neighbouring country had been sentenced to death by the court. The picture of the man standing silently and listening to the judgment flashed repeatedly on the screen. Reaction of world leaders, news analyses, panel discussions expressing hope that the new military ruler may condone the sentence and allow him to leave the country...Ganeshan moved on to a channel covering city news.

There had been a fire in the abandoned factory near Panch Ratan market. It was soon brought under control by the fire brigade helped further by the rain. Still, some of the machines lying idle and the shacks erected by encroachers within the factory's compound were gutted. There had been one death. The reason behind the fire was yet to be ascertained. It was not caused by electricity as power had been disconnected long back. The police were investigating if any extremist elements were involved, perhaps using the premises for making bombs.

A railway employee on duty at the level crossing reported hearing a loud explosion. The factory owner had been taken into custody, and the police were interrogating him.

Rarely did so much happen in one single day. Ganeshan switched off the TV and went inside. He came back with a glass of whisky and stood outside on the veranda watching the sky. There was a gentle breeze. The rain had subsided. White cumulus clouds dotted the sky. The city lights gave them a yellowish glow. Lights would soon start flicking on in houses. The girl in the opposite house would come out to lock the gate. Then she would go inside and switch off the veranda lights. As the city lights mellow, perhaps the clouds may regain their colour, or rather the lack of it, Ganeshan reflected. He closed the front door and went in, only to walk straight up to Aman's room. He opened the windows to let fresh breeze in and sat on the chair in the darkness for some time before switching on the light.

What he read this time was neither a poem nor a song but a prose piece:

Winding up one of my long wanderings that day, I was about to board a bus to return to the town. This had been an extremely tiring expedition, and I was completely exhausted. My backpack on my shoulder, I grabbed the handle bar and was about to pull myself into the bus when I saw an old woman running towards me with a hand raised in air. A large number of people, doubtless evicted from their homes, were camping in the area around the bus station. There were tents pitched and hearths burning. She came from there.

She reached me and caught hold of my shirtsleeve and hung on. Son, are you going to the city, she asked me, as if there is only one city in the world. I said yes.

Her old age was not a gift of time, but of life, I realised as I looked at her face closely. The long flowing garment she wore kind of held her together, it seemed. I realised that she wanted to show me something, and she was in a hurry as my bus was about to leave. Even as one of her hands groped in the pockets of her dress, she held on to my shirtsleeve with the other, as if afraid I would run the moment she let go. She pulled out a scrap of paper from the recesses of her dress. Folded in four, it was the size of a postage stamp. The bus was full now. I waited as she unfolded the paper with her trembling hand, just the one, of course, the other still holding on to my shirtsleeve. Finally, she held it close to my eyes. I took the paper from her and looked at both sides of it. I could see nothing on it. Except grubby crease marks, it was blank. I gave it back to her. Disappointed, the woman put it back in her pocket.

What I failed to see on the paper was the telephone number of her son who had fled to the city to save his life. Again, the city, the abstraction in her mind representing hope and freedom. The number must have been scribbled on it in pencil some time back and could not stand the vagaries of the weather it had passed through. It had faded away. Her eyes all but blind from cataract could not make out anything. But her mind, undimmed, did see and continued to see that telephone number on it. It was now the sole link between she and her son, who had disappeared behind the storms she had passed through. As the bus started moving, she called after me, something I could not catch. She was perhaps giving me her best wishes. I saw a smile momentarily lighting up her eyes, sunken and surrounded by dark shadows. Was it a sudden gush of affection she felt towards me because she thought I was going to 'the city,' where her son lived?

I don't know why she chose me out of all the passengers boarding the bus. Something in my appearance might have reminded her of her son—maybe my age, height, face, or something else. Did that, in turn, give me happiness, the happiness of being the chosen one, chosen by a mother?

I am searching for her son in this city. In this abstraction known as the city, without knowing his name, address, phone number, his age or description…

The next few pages were blank. Ganeshan kept looking at the blank pages for some time, emptying everything from his mind as if to make it as blank as those pages.

FORTY-THREE

Rishi's middle piece on stolen gods came out in the paper. It was written in the form of the strange experience of a duty-minded police officer. The officer had visited the camp of some nomadic people who were generally considered to be thieves, in the course of investigating a case of dacoity. He found no substance in the allegation. On the other hand, he returned with a complaint of theft lodged by the group themselves. The theft of their gods. The officer took the case of stolen gods very seriously, acted promptly and recovered the stolen property from another group's camp. With the gods, a basketful of stones, in his possession, he reached the campsite to return the stolen property, but by that time the complainants had pulled up their tents and disappeared. The gods, now without devotees, lived in the *malkhana* of the police station.

According to Rishi, to the nomads, gods were not protectors but beings to be protected. A godless situation wouldn't leave them helpless and lost but rather feeling robbed of something they cared for. What was God to them? Values, hopes, dreams? There was some absurdity in talking about such things with respect to a people who had no concept of a future. Nomads didn't move in time, they only travelled in space.

But Rishi was of the view that the absence of God might not mean to them the loss of direction, as they didn't feel that they were directed by gods. Rishi reduced all their misfortunes to just losses. During the course of their journey, sometimes some members would go missing. They could have been killed or have fallen dead unbeknownst to them. They could have been taken away by the police and thrown into jails. Or they might have abandoned the journey and joined the community of the settled. Whatever be the case, for them it was a loss. For them, death or destruction were irrelevant. There was only loss. People or gods, stolen from them.

FORTY-FOUR

The police let off the manager of the dhaba after interrogation. They were convinced that he had no role in the factory fire. It also became clear that the fire was not caused by any explosion. There was a barrel full of kerosene among the abandoned things at the factory. Some of the squatters had found it and accidentally set it on fire while trying to get the kerosene out.

The dhaba had changed beyond recognition. Ganeshan saw no crowd there. It was morning when he went there and the kitchen staff were relaxing and gossiping. Some were stretching themselves on the benches meant for customers.

There was a fence separating the ground where refugees camped. Three or four policemen stood guard. The shed where truck drivers used to sleep during overnight halts had been demolished, and the remnants lay scattered. It was now just the dhaba, with the kitchen and an eating area with a few benches and tables. The government was cracking down in the wake of the violence and bomb blasts.

The workers informed him that the manager was out. The dhaba was being closed down, and the authorities had given them only two days to accomplish this, they said. They served him a glass of lassi.

The manager came eventually. He looked calm, like an officer preparing to retire.

'I knew that you would come. I had instructed the workers accordingly,' he said.

'They made me comfortable,' Ganeshan said. 'I was told that the shop is being closed.'

'It has to be. The situation in the city is such. They are also going to seal the refugee camps and keep them under surveillance.'

He sat down on the opposite bench. 'On winter nights, they would assemble here around a fire and sing and dance,' he said nostalgically. 'Each one had his or her own instrument. The boys and girls from good families of the city used to come and join them with their guitars and drums. Those were the good days.'

'Wasn't there danger then?'

'Perhaps there was. Terrorists could easily infiltrate and mingle with them. But when you look at the other side…' he trailed off.

'What are you going to do now?'

'I don't know. One good thing that came of the fire was that the government's attention has been drawn to the case of the factory. If the case is settled, I can sell off the remaining assets. I may leave the city. Go somewhere far away...'

He didn't stay to see off Ganeshan. He went to attend to a customer.

FORTY-FIVE

Aman:
Birds are not bestowed with roots,
Nor trees granted wings.
What the earth holds back only trees can tell,
What the sky deprives only birds know.
The birds perched on the branches
Sing the song of the sky to the trees.
The trees whisper secrets of the earth to the birds.
The birds beg for pardon as they build their nest,
The trees warn the birds as the eggs hatch.
A conversation going on for ages,
Never going anywhere.

FORTY-SIX

The dhaba manager had told Ganeshan that he'd met Koshi only once after the shooting. Koshi desperately wanted to find the woman who had been living with Shamsher, he said. As neighbours and artists, he had a good relationship with the couple. That Vasundhara had left Shamsher before the incident had acquired some meaning in his mind now. The manager had invited Koshi to join him in whatever enterprise he was going to take up. Koshi had not given him any reply. The manager believed that he would return to life gradually when the trauma of the incident subsided.

As if to assert that fortuity was the rule of the world, one day Ganeshan ran into Koshi. While he was waiting for the signal at a crossing, Koshi drove in a tempo and halted just by his side. Ganeshan was a little irritated at the way the driver stopped his vehicle too close to his and when he turned to look at him, it was Koshi! After crossing the junction both of them pulled over into a service lane and stopped to talk.

Koshi looked worn out. The dhaba manager's description of him as a man evicted from life, stage by stage, by events following one after another was writ large not only on his face but all over him. The phenomenon described as the new economic order, the state of individuals falling behind due to their inability to catch up with the fast-moving world, the emergence of self-destructive strife and mindless violence erasing all kinds of reason and faith in society; it appeared all of it had contributed to his state, making him look like one of those buildings in his paintings stripped down to its elements. He was living his art. Against his wishes, Ganeshan's eyes lingered on the tattered clothes, greying and dishevelled hair, dry and cracking lips. Why, didn't Koshi look so even when he first met him in the factory, Ganeshan thought to himself. Even then he had appeared fractured and shattered. Perhaps because he was surrounded by his work that depicted destruction and collapse, it didn't appear so. But now there were no creative works around him. An old, noisy, smoke-spitting three-wheeler stood by his side.

Koshi actually did not sound depressed. His van was loaded with food. He was now a driver for one of the vans that collect left-over food from star hotels, airports, railway canteens and private parties and take to prescribed centres around the city, where it would be distributed among street children. The idea, when floated by a social service organisation working among street children, received immediate support and cooperation from the hotel industry. Koshi himself looked excited when he spoke of it. 'Can you imagine the wastage? Now all that surplus food that used to be thrown into garbage dumps feeds hundreds of children!' he said. For Koshi, it was like a free service; he was paid a small pocket money, enough to meet his needs. 'What else do I need now?' he asked.

Ganeshan reminded him of the dhaba manager's offer to which his reply was a smile.

'Your flat...' Ganeshan didn't know what further to ask about it.

'What was left to me were my wife and daughter,' Koshi said as if his mind was elsewhere. 'The job had gone, income too. It had become difficult to keep the house. To be frank, it had become difficult even to feed the family. Still, in my state, they were my biggest assets. It was only when I lost them that I realised I had actually become a pauper long back. I had then no other alternative than to leave the house.'

'The police have taken custody of it, they said. Not that they don't know the tragedy that struck you. But your disappearance so soon after the incident and that you were close to Shamsher, all together...'

'What amazes me, Ganeshan, is that while everything collapses, gets divided and fragmented, somewhere these fragments come together. As the threads of events unravel, they also roll up elsewhere. Does deconstruction follow construction, or is it the other way round? Can the criminal investigation department solve this enigma?'

'Who knows, Koshi. The threads of logic and evidence the investigators use as warp and woof to weave their stories also play a part in the grand design of the fabric around us. The gruesome tragedy at the marriage party, the inhuman compulsions working in the minds of terrorists, the burnt out factory, the dhaba, the dhaba owner, your art, all apparently so unrelated, but the blood and tears flowing through them all work like threads pulling them all into one design. Questions such as which is the woof and which the warp have little relevance.'

Koshi slowly nodded. 'Isn't there a saying that neighbours are more important than relatives?' he asked. 'They were living right next door. We shared a common wall. If we drove a nail into it, dust would fall in their room. I was shattered, Ganeshan. The wall, which was not a wall, the nail, the dust… Vasundhara had already left Shamsher. Perhaps she would be able to answer my questions.'

Ganeshan saw the picture of buildings collapsed in earthquakes again. Pages Cawasji tore from the register, the numbers on them, the photographs, all joined them on the wall. An exhibition is perhaps completed only when the nails are driven into the wall, when dust falls.

'The word displaced has a number of connotations, Koshi,' said Ganeshan. 'There won't be any use in your meeting Vasundhara. Her mind has retreated behind the walls of reason. She is a prisoner to insanity now.'

Koshi stared at Ganeshan quietly for some time. Then he suddenly exclaimed as if just remembering, 'Oh, my God, I am getting late. I have to take this food to the centre before it becomes stale. It comes to us as old stuff, you know.'

Koshi hurriedly got into the driver's seat and started the vehicle.

Ganeshan looked at the piece of paper Koshi had thrust into his hand. It had his address, an unauthorised colony of workers retrenched from their jobs.

FORTY-SEVEN

Why did the newspaper do away with its Saturday feature, *City Notebook*, Ganeshan wondered. The feature used to tell the stories of ordinary people, sometimes even animals, which did not have any political significance. It could not have been a policy decision. Perhaps the writer of the column moved to another publication. They will restart it as soon as they find a replacement, he told himself. But it's been a month, and that has not happened.

The last feature to appear had been about the death of a five-year old girl in a slum cluster. The columnist had suggested that the piece, horrifying as it was, could serve as the advertisement of a soft drink brand. A resident of the colony, perhaps a labourer, snatched two soft drink bottles from man who had come to deliver the bottles to the shops there. The supplier protested and left only to return with some elders to admonish the labourer. An argument ensued leading to a physical fight between the man and the elders.

A crowd gathered and in the melee, a five-year old girl was trampled to death. It was unfortunate that the feature series ended with such a macabre story, Ganeshan felt.

Instead of restarting the feature, after some time, the paper allotted the space to another column called *Urban V-Scape*, V for violence. Small human-interest stories still took place in the city. But they have now made way for big violence. Bigger violence basically trampled smaller ones to death.

Sometime after the massacre at the wedding party, the city witnessed a full-scale communal riot that took the lives of fifty people. A number of houses were torched and a house of worship was gutted. This was followed within a few days by two car bomb blasts, discovery of a huge cache of weapons and explosives, killings of film stars for blood money, busting of a drug racket and a human trafficking gang. All topped off by protests by liberation activists. The usurping of the *City Notebook* feature by *Urban V-Scape* appeared fully justified.

There were also plenty of other irritants for the city administration, like fires in expensive high-rise buildings, burning landfills, dengue fever, pollution and adulterated cooking oil leading to paralysing nerve damage in consumers. There were demands for an overhaul of city administration, a re-examination of urban policies and a whole new action plan to be drawn up.

It was in these circumstances that the commissioner's phone call came. He called from his home. Perhaps with a drink in hand, relaxing on his veranda, after a long day of meetings with politicians and confrontation with young, hungry reporters. The commissioner was an old friend. A soft-spoken, but a bold and decisive man.

'It is a long time since we have seen you, Ganeshan,' the commissioner said.

'Yes, I have shifted to another camp,' Ganeshan said.

'Consider it a camp only then. I know the circumstances of your retirement. But life continues. Come meet me once, for the sake of old friendship.'

Ganeshan said with a smile in his voice, 'What do you want from me?'

'Come to the office tomorrow. Around eleven?'

'I will come, but tell me the purpose.'

'You are very well aware of the situation. Your experience would be of help to us.'

Though not happy about it, Ganeshan could not say no.

FORTY-EIGHT

The catch-up between friends turned out to be a full-scale meeting, there were representatives of the city corporation, state government, police department and intelligence. The original cause and the ultimate solutions of course lay elsewhere, but the city commissioner is the one who eventually has to deal with the fallouts in the city.

It was while sitting in the meeting that Ganeshan realised how the period after his retirement from service has influenced his mind and shaped his attitudes. He used to spend long hours in this very committee room with his files and notes and having these discussions, but now he felt suffocated. Although the air outside was no better.

Apprehensions regarding the unchecked influx of non-citizens into the city came from usual quarters. Concerns Ganeshan himself had expressed several times while sitting in these chairs. The circumstances he had expatiated umpteen times were again elaborated. The argument was that poor people, who migrated to the city from villages in long gone days, used to easily get integrated with it, but the current migrants could not establish an organic relationship with the city, and they always remained outsiders. That they, in mind and in action, belonged elsewhere; that they were only using the city to their advantage.

Ganeshan had to finally interrupt the flow and point out that there was no use complaining about things upon which one had no control. When we know it was not possible to solve the problems, the best course of action is to figure out ways to keep engaging with them continuously, so that they do not overwhelm us.

The police and intelligence were as usual at loggerheads. Cases were being solved by clues discovered fortuitously rather than on systematic investigation, it was alleged. Constable Chunni Ram's findings were quoted as an example. This was countered by allegations that intelligent intelligence was also very rare to come by. The surprising connections emerging between different cases failed to resolve into rational evidence and were allowed to relapse as mysteries. It was pointed out that the departments were losing the people's confidence at a time when their cooperation was needed the most. The public which lost confidence in the system was as dangerous as criminals, because they unwittingly ended up aiding them.

Official positions and interpretations were like boats without oars floating aimlessly in water, Ganeshan argued. They were incapable of measuring the depth of the river or taking you across it. Chunni Rams should not be derided. Mysteries and fortuities had always been our stable companions. Finding solutions to problems had never been the work of agencies. Their ingenuity lay in converting apparently negative outcomes into positive opportunities.

The meeting ended with a decision to have another meeting, a massive brainstorming, in a couple days. The fallout of the meeting for Ganeshan was a proposal from the Commissioner for him to continue engaging with the effort in the capacity of an adviser.

'No Commissioner, I am not for it.'

'The administration has no choice but to continue with its efforts Ganeshan, even if we seem to be going in circles.'

'Certainly, I am not arguing against it. The government must carry out its duties. Only my mind is now on another track, commisioner. I don't have any immediate solutions or ideas for the problems. All I have is a different mindset.'

'I noticed that change in mindset. I am trying to make use of that.'

'Should everything take place through the commissioner and the government only?'

'No, certainly not,' the commissioner agreed.

'Our architect friend Cawasji says that every disaster originates in accounting. That bookkeeping imprisons truth behind the prison cell-like bars of the account books. He has a point but we still need accounting, bookkeeping. When there is such large-scale displacement and movement of people, we are forced to take account of them. But...'

'Yes, go on.'

'I'm afraid this is not the place for discussing all that.'

'If it is?'

Ganeshan searched his mind for the right words. Struggles aimed at creating and establishing identity is what leads to uprooting and loss of identity. Every year presents us a with a new set of boat people or camp people, uprooted, peripatetic, borne out of identity reinforcements by others. The result seems to be the opposite of the original purpose, goal. To the extent that one is left wondering about the purpose itself. In fact what is happening is the ultimate destruction of cause or purpose. Lives, movements, actions are tending towards purposelessness.

'But you said that we have no alternative than to face the situation.'

'Yes. Facing them, and through facing them, how to convert the negative situations into positive ones. The question is how we can re-discover happiness. In a situation bereft of happiness, in fact we have removed happiness from the agenda. We may have to go back to the foundations. We may have to take down some of the burdens we call culture from our shoulders to be able to regain our mobility.'

The commissioner's silence invited more elaboration.

'We look at everything as numbers when we are sitting on the side of administration,' Ganeshan continued. 'Seeing the forest and not the trees, so to speak. The cavemen could not do math, yet the chiefs did keep a count of the tribe. Perhaps by seeing each member individually and separately.'

'What are you doing now, Ganeshan?'

'I don't know, to be frank. What I have realised is that there are vantage points other than those of the government for looking at society. To tell the truth, what I have in my hand now are a few individuals. Some present, some missing, some I have never met, some may not even exist.'

Ganeshan laughed. But the commissioner knew that it was not mirth. He did not join in the laughter.

FORTY-NINE

No sooner had Ganeshan reached home than the Mission's van pulled up at the gate. Naseema got down and exchanged their special greeting. He has seen them exchanging it every time they met or parted.

Naseema looked tired, but happy and contented. Summer was withdrawing, and the fan was on at a slow speed in the room. After stepping in, Naseema paused, looked around and gave him and the house a smile. Did the house appear new to her?

She accepted the glass of water he brought. He extended his hand to take her luggage, but she refused to give it to him, with another smile. She took the things into her room and returned. As she sat on the sofa, Ganeshan came up behind her and placed his hands on her shoulder. As if suddenly reminded, she sprang up and embraced him.

'This was a new chapter in my life,' she said, unable to tamp down her excitement.

'What was?'

'Everything. The meditation, recitation, prayer. Do you know, Ganeshan, that the prayer hall of the ashram has no idols? The prayer itself was nothing but recitation of stanzas from Upanishads, no mention of a god. In a way, everything is a prayer there. Meditation, recitation, cooking, washing, gardening…'

Ganeshan nodded in agreement. 'There are innumerable practices of worship in the Hindu system. There is freedom to make new ones, too. Even new gods. That is why newer and newer missions and sects keep appearing.'

'You are on to your old tricks again, Ganeshan,' Naseema said.

Ganeshan laughed sheepishly.

'I must take a bath now,' said Naseema, dismissing him. 'Mountains are so fresh. Plains generate dust, dust of all hues.'

Ganeshan went into his room with the papers handed over to him in the meeting. Background paper and other attachments. He didn't read them there. Nor was he in a mind to read them now. Leaving them on the table, he stretched out on the bed. The sunlight filtering in through the window had something sad about it. Lengthening sunrays and lengthening shadows. He dozed off.

In the evening, Naseema went out to meet some friends in the neighbourhood. Ganeshan went for a walk. The late night

TV was showing an old film, and they watched it together for some time. Then they switched to a news channel. The panel discussions on the death sentence on the displaced prime minister continued. It looked like that the military dictator would accede to international pressure and allow him to take asylum abroad. Surprisingly, the public and the media of the country itself did not seem quite interested in the matter. At the home front, as usual, scandals and scams occupied the space.

Naseema kept interjecting with descriptions of the beautiful places she visited. It was already quite cold in the mountains. She talked about the forests as if she had seen them for the first time. One day the swami took them along a walking trail that wound up the hills. At one place they sat down, and the swami talked to them about the intimate relationship human beings have with other beings on earth, the animals and trees. The water in the stream flowing past the ashram was ice-cold because it was snowmelt from the peaks higher up. There was another trail on the rear side of the ashram, which at a particular turn brings one face to face with a valley deep down. The high cliff and precipice with the forlorn valley down below should inspire awe in one's mind but surprisingly it only captivated one with its magical way. He was captivated by her descriptions, Ganeshan confessed.

After the news, the channel started showing the live telecast of a cricket match. The room was suddenly filled with the din of the stadium. Naseema retired to her room, wishing Ganeshan good night. He lowered the volume but still the noise continued.

There was a commotion in the stadium. The agitation and excitement of the audience and heated discussion between the commentators indicated that there was a sort of crisis in the game. Soon it became clear from the repeated replay shots. It was an unusual situation. After hitting the ball, the batsman had begun to run. The other batsman also did the same. But when both of them reached the centre of the pitch, there was a confusion as to whether they should complete the run or return to their wickets. As they paused in indecision at the centre of the pitch, a fielder hit the stumps on one side. The confusion of the batsmen, celebration of the fielders, commotion in the galleries, screams of the commentators and above all, the consultation among the umpires as to which batsman should be declared out, flashed across the screen turn by turn. As the decision was delayed, both batsmen remained at the centre of the pitch embarrassed and wondering which was their home, the one they had left or the one they were aiming to reach. At last, the decision came; but the technical solution was survived by the unique philosophical aspects of the situation. The batsman declared out walked towards the pavilion, but the other one was still in a stupor and both wickets remained unoccupied.

Ganeshan thought it was the right point to leave the game. Switching off the TV, he climbed the stairs to Aman's room.

A feeling that he talked too much at the commissioner's chamber lingered on in his mind. Naseema's return made him happy. But gradually, it was dawning on him that their paths were diverging, and she was moving away from him. It was perhaps unwarranted. But feeling happy about someone coming closer to one did not seem meaningless at all. Yet the question remained, which is our home, the one we left behind or the one we are aiming to reach? All those who are alive are forever in such a state. We are travellers, always. Neither he nor Naseema had a special status in this. Special statuses were reserved for those who died. But did they also not die en route?

Aman had written:

I watch the sunlight
Entering through the window and
Falling on my floor,
Splintered lengthwise and across
Against the grilles of the window
Into squares of light.
When I see the squares growing smaller
And slanting on one side,
Elongating to become rectangles,

Forming parallelograms,
Thinning and thinning
To end as lines,
Separate and lonely,
I feel that they have life in them,
That they are living beings,
That their lives are ending.

Then he had written another line and crossed it out in a way that it could not be read. After that, another blank page.

Ganeshan closed the drawer and opened the window facing the vacant plot. The light falling on the ground through the window didn't change its shape. The squares remained stable. After all, it was dead.

FIFTY

Ganeshan woke up with a feeling that he was late in rising. The feeling seemed to be present even in his sleep. It was a sign of uneasy sleep. Wakefulness sandwiched in sleep itself.

Further proof to his rising late were the squares of sunlight on the floor. He watched those squares with some awe. And as he watched them, they shortened and slanted to one side according to the sun's position.

Evidence of life in a thing should stimulate one, not create awe. But it can create uneasiness, even guilt when you discover life in something, which you had thought lifeless. When you watch that life draining out, it turns to awe.

Naseema appeared at the door, with a cup of tea.

'I would have come there,' he said.

That was the practice. Coffee and tea at the coffee table.

'Some practices should be broken, sometimes,' she said.

'It is good to do that,' he agreed.

Later, when they met at the table, Ganeshan put the morning paper down and said, 'Do you remember Naseema, a girl who sent a birthday greetings card to you once? Long back, along with a landscape of Cézanne? We had a small fight over that. That girl is coming to see us.'

'Really?' Naseema remembered her, but there was not much interest in her voice. She didn't ask who the girl was or how Ganeshan came to know of her.

Ganeshan tried to explain, 'Zoya is her name. She had gone to meet Rishi. She told him that she would come see us. She was close to Aman she said.'

'Sure. How else would it be?' Naseema gave a laugh. 'See, results.'

Results of what, Ganeshan wanted to ask but didn't. She wanted to credit that happiness, too, to the meditation.

'Aman used to write poems, Naseema, really good poems,' he said again.

'Yes, not surprising given his nature.'

The indifference in her voice pained him. She didn't even want to see them. Ganeshan didn't pursue the matter further. Nor did she ask anything more.

Ganeshan finished his tea and went out to the garden. Naseema had survived Aman, he realised.

The sunlight falling on the ground was not divided into squares. It was just light spread on flat ground.

FIFTY-ONE

'The story was not even of stolen gods, it was of obsolete gods, that is what I am realising now.' That is how Rishi started. There was a satisfaction on his face, of being able to solve at least one small part of the mystery. He continued ponderingly, 'This idea created with a liberal mix of colours of strangeness and mystery might very well have such a dimension, too, of obsolescence!'

Ganeshan had not yet recovered from the confusion created by Rishi's middle page article. And here he was opening up another chapter. The cycle of losing, re-gaining and losing again had become a part of his existence. Was Rishi now introducing yet another cycle, concentric cycles of obsolescence, renewal and obsolescence again?

They were nursing a beer each in a small restaurant on top of a hillock; it was a mildly warm afternoon. The window opened towards a temple in the distance. They could see the decorations and the crowd of a fair there, which had not ended, though Janmashtami was a more than a month ago. The music from the speakers, although weakened by the distance, still reached them.

The child god stolen away from the jail must have already started growing up with his new parents, Ganeshan reflected. He was born in summer. There was another god, born in the peak of winter, also deported and exchanged hands as a child. He was not just brought up in alien hands, his fatherhood itself remained enmeshed in mystery! Was he God or only God's son? His birth marked the coming of a new year; a new era itself. Year after year, season after season, these legends were reenacted and celebrated as if gods were born, stolen, dead and resurrected time and again.

'Four or five years back, a Banjara boy was caught by police for some petty offence,' Rishi continued. 'Somehow, Saathi got involved. Saathi means Vasundhara. She couldn't free him. Before that, the court had sent him off to a reformatory. He was lost in the darkness of it.'

'Vijay?' Ganeshan became anxious.

'No, insofar as the facts go,' said Rishi. 'Of course, only Vasundhara can vouch for it. She was handling the case almost single-handedly.'

Rishi had met Vasundhara twice, but he could not communicate with her. Taking advantage of his relationship with Saathi, he talked to some of the older members. What he could gather was that the boy had handed over a basketful of stones, round-shaped and of different hues, to Vasundhara before he was taken away by the police. She brought them to the office of Saathi. The boy had requested her to hand them over to his people. Vasundhara tried to comply with the boy's request, said Vineeta. She had accompanied Vasundhara when she went in search of the camps of Banjaras. It was to no avail; the group had left the site long back. She could not trace them. Due to her guilt, she stopped visiting the boy.

'It must be those stones that Naseema took home,' Rishi said. 'Vasundhara didn't object as she could do nothing more for them. She had only told Naseema that the stones were the gods of a Banjara group. A hard rationalist, Vasundhara didn't think the beliefs around them were of any importance to modern people like her and Naseema.'

'Quite some time later, once in Saathi, Vasundhara revealed more about the beliefs of the nomadic tribes. As it was obligatory for the nomadic tribes to keep changing their locations, she said that it was also customary for them to renew their gods. Stones of different colours and shapes collected from beds of streams were their gods. They travelled with such gods in their baskets and renewed them every year. In the month of Kartika or so, when the water in rivers receded, they collected new stones from the riverbeds to replace the old ones that they discard.* For that purpose,

*Kartika is the eighth month of the Hindu calendar which falls between October and November of the Gregorian calendar

they camped near streams in those months. If they didn't do so, they believed that the gods in their baskets would turn into devils. All this she came to know from the boy in the reformatory. Elizabeth remembers that Vasundhara told her once that the boy had escaped from the home and visited her. Since the stones in the basket had already turned into devils in the meanwhile, he didn't take them back. If what Elizabeth says is true, the boy was not Vijay by any means.'

Rishi returned to his beer. The speakers from the temple had gone silent, and the merry-go-rounds in the fair had become still.

'Janmashtami is over,' said Ganeshan. 'Christmas is coming. Gods of us settled people also often needed human protection to save them from wicked ones! But they were never lost to us totally.'

'Except for rationalists,' said Rishi, returning to the story. 'Ganeshan, Vasundhara was Vasundhara. Like all rationalists, she, too, thought that others thought like her. In a merry mood, she seems to have told Naseema that the basket she had taken home was full of devils for they had not been renewed in time. Naseema exploded at that. She shouted at her, asking why she didn't tell her that beforehand. It was during that time that Aman had died. In her state of mind, she may have feared that the tragedy that fell on your family was all conjured up by the devils in her own garden. That she herself had been instrumental in Aman's death.

She accused Vasundhara that she had intentionally suppressed the information from her though she had known the beliefs of the nomads. Vineeta says this was not true, Vasundhara learned all this much later. But Vasundhara didn't argue with Naseema or justify herself, perhaps in deference to Naseema's loss. According to others, she just went totally pale and withdrew into silence. Naseema stopped going to Saathi after that incident, they say. Vasundhara also was deeply affected by it, and her friends say that she has not laughed wholeheartedly after that.'

Rishi asked for a refill to fill the silence that suddenly fell into the space between them than their nearly full mugs.

'Poor Naseema,' said Ganeshan lowering his voice as if he was speaking to himself. 'It must be the embarrassment of succumbing to superstition that prevented her from telling me all this. She carried all that pain and guilt inside her alone. The intensity of the loss drove her to superstition. She must have sought refuge in total faith to escape from the power of superstition. Now she has become completley spiritual. Not just Saathi, she is not going to the magazine's office even. The only place she goes, and there she goes every day without fail, is the ashram of the swami. Vasundhara, too, seems to have found refuge in…'

Ganeshan fell silent. Rishi was looking out where the fair had come alive once again.

They left the restaurant and drove to Ganeshan's house.

Naseema was not home. The slip under the plate of spoons on the coffee table said that a friend from Saathi had come, and she was going out with her to the Neurology Centre where Vasundhara had been admitted.

'Let us see those stones once more,' Rishi said.

To their surprise, they saw that the hanging branches of bougainvillea were cut, and the whole area had been cleared. Neither the stones nor the basket was there. Peering out over the compound wall, Ganeshan saw that they had been thrown out. Stones, basket, all. To the vacant plot, behind which they lay scattered among the shrubs.

Ganeshan and Rishi came back to the front veranda and sat down. The sun had already moved to the back of the house.

'Just like Vasundhara's rationalism shoved them away as unimportant, now Naseema's faith, too, has banished those stones out of her doors,' Ganeshan said. 'Besides faith and rationalism, there must be some other space available to us, don't you think so, Rishi? The original custodians of the stones—the Banjara group—have moved on to their new abodes, abandoning them. The boy, too, didn't want to take them as they have turned into devils…Naseema and Vasundhara have both embarked on journeys from which there may be no return. Are these stones turning everybody who has come in contact with them into nomads?'

'The path on which you are now travelling is that third path, Ganeshan. It is known as the path of imagination!'

'Imagination now takes my mind to another person. To a boy called Vijay. The boy, after suffering such a violent end, has disappeared so completely from everywhere. The nomadic blood running through his veins forced him to jump the walls of Ashaniketan. He didn't succeed and ended up as pulp. We do not have even some stones with us to call his. There is a collection of photos of which we do not know which one is his. Presented to us by Cawasji. And he keeps enlarging that collection.'

'There is one more thing with us, Ganeshan. A small piece of paper in the files of the police where your name is written.'

'I don't know what that small piece of paper signifies. I am wondering what it has done. It has set me on a path where more and more people are joining me, but no one is able to tell me where it leads.'

'This third path, Ganeshan, it has no answers which rationalism is always keen to give. Nor will it offer you the peace that spirituality has rewarded Naseema. But that is the fate of our times. Answers and peace are to be found only in the realm of imagination.'

'Rishi, in your article you speak about the nomads putting all their worries in the basket of losses. What they carry is actually a basket of losses. We are not nomads and unlike them, time is very much a presence to us. Still, we, too, are sitting with our basket of losses in our laps.'

'Gods turning into devils or being stolen, it is all actually about failure of renewal. Theft closes the possibility of renewal. What is actually stolen is the possibility of renewal. You are right. Strains of nomadism have crept into us, our city lives. We have no permanent gods, no permanent relations or permanent solutions. Still, we find difficulty in coming to terms with the idea of obsolescence. The idea of obsolete gods turning against us as devils. The idea that obsolescence is, in one way, coming to terms with the times.'

'Once, at our dinner table, I'd mentioned how each city was considered to have a *nagar devta* or diety whose temple used to stand at the centre of the city. Naseema had then said that citizens have abandoned the city goddess at the centre and are going in all directions in search of the ever-eluding goddess of growth. Suddenly, Aman had thrown in the question, who was a citizen? No city belonged to citizens, as we define it nowadays, he'd said. That the very idea of a citizen was an illusion. According to him, cities belonged to those who come from outside it every day. We talk about citizens, the permanent dwellers of the city, while the very idea of a permanent dweller is evaporating, turning into a myth. That word, like our world, is breaking up. I think I can now understand the meaning of what Aman had said then.'

'There are so many things about Aman that you haven't told me.'

'Rishi, a moment ago you mentioned the piece of paper they found in Vijay's bag. A small living piece of paper that was left behind by the dead boy. Aman had also told me about a similar piece of paper. A piece of paper folded into four the size of a postage stamp. You should hear this.'

And Ganeshan started telling Rishi that story.

FIFTY-TWO

Why did Rishi become so vocal about the idea of permanent relations and permanent solutions when these things were disappearing from the minds of modern citizens? The question confronted Ganeshan's mind when news of Seeta's violent death came.

That was the way Seeta chose to surface after hiding herself from everyone for such a long period. In the form of a body, the life of which was snuffed out instantly by one bullet that passed through her heart. Killed in the ambience of a farmhouse restaurant, before the eyes of the cream of the city assembled there to enjoy a Saturday evening.

Everyone thought that Rishi would collapse. Even Naseema, lost in the mystic world of the swami, was shaken. Ganeshan who had not seen Seeta even once struggled to come to terms with it. Rishi was certainly shaken when she disappeared all of a sudden, with a kind of defiance and arrogance, the purpose of which was not clear to anybody.

Then he adjusted himself to the situation and appeared to have prepared himself to face anything. He talked about her lesser and lesser, till he finally stopped it altogether. He looked for distractions like investigating the story behind the stones in Naseema's garden. Once Ganeshan remarked to Naseema that he was putting up a brave face. Naseema said that behind that face was the same Rishi.

It all happened in the small hours after midnight. The farmhouse was a vast complex, which included a few cottages for stay, a sprawling garden, a lake, a yoga centre and even a cave for meditation, besides of course the famous restaurant. It was common knowledge that the place belonged to the don Kaku Supplier, but the ownership of the place was not a question of any interest to the fun-seekers. The media advertised the famous Saturday Enclaves in the restaurant, and the gossip columns of the city pages of newspapers told you of the VIPs, artists, business magnates and intellectuals who graced the gathering each Saturday. Cultural events like Rajasthani folk dances and Baul music which added splendour to the evenings never went unreported. How Seeta could be working as a bar girl at the place was beyond anyone's comprehension.

The party was going on full swing. Away from the hubbub of the city, slopes of hills, banks of a lake and shade of trees, moonlight, cool breeze and above all, the relaxed mood of a Saturday evening provided enough for fun, games and romance. All were in a good mood. But as per the rules, the bar closed at twelve, sharp. Those who wanted to carry on with the party would have already bought enough drinks in advance.

At ten past twelve, four young men appeared from nowhere. They went straight to the bar and asked for drinks. They were already pretty drunk. Seeta who was at the counter at the time showed them the sign, 'Bar Closed'. They shoved the sign out of the way and demanded to be served. When Seeta declined again, one of them whipped out a revolver and shot her. As the victim collapsed behind the bar, the assailants coolly got into their vehicle and left the place.

Except that her name was Seeta, nobody there knew anything about her. It was only her second day there. Ganeshan, Naseema and Rishi reached the hospital after reading about the incident in the newspaper—they had published details of her driving license. There was no one else there to identify her. No one from her previous or current workplace. Her adoptive parents had already moved out to their hometown long back. The police were trying to reach them, from the information supplied by Rishi. Seeta had lived her whole life in this city, but when dead, there were only these three people who said they knew her.

It took the whole day to get the body released after the autopsy. Since there were no relatives present, the authorities moved it to the mortuary after allowing them to see and identify her. They returned to Ganeshan's house.

After two days' efforts, the police succeeded in tracing Seeta's parents. But the aged couple showed no interest in coming to the city and receiving the body. Ganeshan, Naseema and Rishi again approached the police for claiming the body. To the officer's question, 'who are you to the dead person?' Rishi's spontaneous reply was 'everything.' This irritated the officer. When asked for her address, Rishi had no answer. He had only silence to offer to her employment details. He couldn't even tell her age. It was only then he realised that the person whom he loved with all his heart was so far removed from him. Tired, at last he gave up, saying, 'Yes, I don't know anything about her, but she had only me.'

Ganeshan approached inspector Tarun Kumar. He promptly arrived, but after taking stock of the situation, advised that there was no other way than to submit to the rules. Especially given the intriguing circumstances in which she was killed. After waiting for a specific period, according to the rules, the authorities would themselves cremate her body. They would intimate them at the time. They can be present in the crematorium.

That was how Seeta ended. Strange girl. She didn't have any respect for relationships. At the age of two, she showed up at a police station from the street. Kept at bay all those who wanted to make her theirs or love her. Taught others the meaninglessness of human relationships. Although she landed right in the middle of a firefight between two mafia gangs, she was killed mindlessly by an inebriated stranger angry at not being served. Cremated by the police as an unclaimed body.

Rishi regained equilibrium very easily. He did not make any attempt to find out where Seeta had been living or where she was working or how she happened to land in a place like that. He left all that to the police to find out. The policemen kept coming to him for some time with questions. He told them all that he knew but did not want to be party to the investigation. There was no use, he said. It was the truth that was in the end punished in the courts. There won't be any witnesses to provide evidence. A murder that took place in full view of the powerful in the city would ultimately be written off as one committed in total solitude, away from the sight of all living beings.

Naseema returned to her meditation classes and spiritual discourses of the swami. Ganeshan to his friends and neighbours. Rishi started taking more interest in his research. He intensified his efforts to go abroad for continuing the work. He wanted to go to Australia. One or two middles of his appeared in newspapers during that period. Both were unconnected to his subject, anthropology, and were meant for light reading. One was about the ostentatious marriage practices among the rich of the city where teasing the bride's party by the bridegrooms' party had become an essential ritual. The groom's procession would start from his house at the right time and would take forever to reach the wedding venue, where the bride's party waited. The other was about the clusters of slums mushrooming every day, offering opportunities to competing political parties for protecting them. The protection work ultimately goes to the highest bidder. They had tempting and meaningful names like No Man's Land or Take-It-Or-Leave-It. He had discovered the existence of real slum clusters with those names, he said.

FIFTY-THREE

There was a bottleneck in the road due to a historic tomb right in the middle of it, on the road divider. Immediately after it, there was a traffic light. Together they created regular traffic congestion. In the evening, the line of vehicles would stretch interminably. In addition to that, today a bus was attempting a U-turn. Ganeshan switched off the engine and rested his legs.

Two beautiful tall buildings had come up on the right side of the road. That portion of the land had been planned as a new plaza. A spacious square with fountains, trees and benches, had already taken shape with business buildings and shopping complexes outlining it. There used to be an old cinema, reflecting a mix of gothic and early European architecture, in that area previously. It was an opera house initially, which was converted into a cinema when operas became obsolete. Now, even that was being dismantled. Some interested citizens had filed a public interest case in the court pleading for the preservation of the building as a heritage structure, which was rejected. Its status as a monument was lost long back when it was converted into a cinema hall, the court observed.

The roof of the hall had gone. Walls were standing high inspiring awe among onlookers. A long flight of stairs abruptly ended in the air. It was not known what would come up in its place. People speculated. On the footpath, Tibetan refugees had spread out their wares, soft woollen clothes in preparation of the impending winter.

The vehicles started moving again, and Ganeshan followed the ones before him. A few minutes, he would be out of it and can enjoy the freedom, he consoled himself. He had come out just for that, to enjoy freedom from the crowd, to breath some fresh air and to have the pleasure of driving along empty roads. It was the road leading to the countryside, out of the city.

Soon the traffic thinned. Fields appeared on either side of the road. The evening had painted the clouds red near the horizon. Summer had already retreated, and autumn too was following suit. There was a freshness and chill in the air. He parked the car on the side of the road and got out.

Vast fields bared after harvest lay before him. There was total silence except a distant call or cry. Stubble after the harvest had been put to fire at one place and smoke from it rose to the sky. He walked towards a cluster of huts visible a little ahead by the side of the road.

A huge peepul tree on the side of the road played host to a small shrine underneath it. The shrine was actually the tomb of some holy person. The tree stood touching the tomb and a kind of makeshift shelter had been built for the tomb by providing a slanting roof from the trunk of the tree. A Devanagari signboard painted in white over a green background, by an inexperienced painter said: Dargah Sharif Hazrat Gular Shahvali. There was nobody around. Someone had left incense sticks burning. A small metal sheet nailed to the tree exhorted against inserting sandal sticks on the tree trunk and causing it pain. In a hollow of the tree trunk, a piece of mirror broken from a larger one was placed. The mirror appeared to be the object of worship there. Incense was burning in front of it. Ganeshan bent before it and looked at his reflection on it. Though the piece of mirror was small, one could get the full picture of the face by adjusting one's distance or shifting to both sides. The message of the holy man lying buried there had perhaps something to do with reflections.

Ganeshan turned back from the shrine, abandoning the idea of going to the village ahead. The sun had set. It was getting cold. He touched his face with his cold palms and found it pleasing.

FIFTY-FOUR

Darkness set in as he drove back. Fields were left behind and soon he reached crowded roads, bordered by shops. Then the shops gave way to wayside workshops, the vehicles awaiting repair and dumps of tires encroaching upon the road menacingly. Ganeshan took another road forking out of the main. He was sure that it would join the main road as he knew the area very well.

This road was relatively less crowded and there were even stretches with practically no human presence. Then, the shops and bazaars reappeared and again lonely stretches. Gradually it dawned on him that the road was not familiar to him. The landmarks he was expecting did not appear. To add to the confusion, the power went off suddenly, leaving the road, shops and houses in total darkness. The headlights of vehicles the only source of light. A few lights fed by captive generators blinked their eyes here and there, but they were of little help. Ganeshan went on driving with a growing sense of unease.

A government residential colony appeared on the left side. The yellow walls were faintly visible even in the darkness. On the opposite side were tall modern apartments, privately owned. Some of them had light, but the government colony was still in darkness.

Some activity was going on inside the colony even in darkness. A patch of dust was rising in the air at a distance, which could be seen in the floodlights commissioned for the work. Noise of machines whirring could also be heard.

The colony looked familiar to Ganeshan, and he had a feeling that he had lived there once. It must have been one of the several places Ganeshan and Naseema lived during the long service years. Even without his realising, he turned into the road approaching the colony.

A short drive through the interior roads, and it was clear that the colony was empty. The headlights of his car turning left and right like the searchlights showed that the houses were uninhabited. No noise came from anywhere except the distant roar of machines. The roads were empty and so were the grounds between houses where children would play and old people take their evening rounds. Here the lights were off perhaps due to the disconnection of power rather than the failure of it. Under the starlight, the colony presented an eerie look. Ganeshan slowly drove in the direction of the machinic noises.

The sound of the generator dominated everything else. Floodlights lit up the area. Two cranes with booms were at work. Huge iron wrecking balls suspended from the booms were being used to demolish the flats. Ganeshan got out of the car and and stood watching the operation with awe. There were not many workers on the site. Only a few supervisors appeared to be about shouting instructions to the operators through the din of the machines. When the balls hit the structures, the whole ground seemed to shake.

The buildings did not appear to be in a bad condition. They were not that old either. Why were they being pulled down? Since the residents of the whole colony had been evacuated and the buildings made vacant, the plan was perhaps to demolish the entire colony. The idea sent a chill down Ganeshan's spine.

The next hit brought down a sizable chunk of walls and floors. The dust it raised filled the whole sky and for some time blinded his vision. When the dust settled, the booms of cranes swung again.

Ganeshan suddenly saw Cawasji emerging from the settling dust. Cawasji waved at Ganeshan and gestured him to wait. He spent a few seconds to talk to the supervisors, then started walking towards him.

Cawasji didn't ask Ganeshan how he happened to be there. He spoke as if he knew he would come.

'Three months' time has been given. Will be sufficient, I think,' said Cawasji.

'To demolished the whole colony?' Ganeshan asked, as if he had already accepted that the colony was to be taken down.

'Exactly.'

'So many houses. When there is such an acute shortage of houses…'

Not trying to reply to his comment, Cawasji continued with what he wanted to say, 'This is a pilot project. Of dismantling permanent houses and building temporary ones in their place. If the idea is found workable, other colonies also would be notified. All colonies.'

'What?'

'Once we have taken a road, we should go the full distance. Isn't it?'

'Not necessarily, Cawasji. What are the turns and junctions for? In fact, I reached this place by taking an unexpected turn from my usual route.'

Cawasji didn't reply to that either. Instead, he shifted to another topic. 'This is also an opportunity for us to study the construction.' He paused a few seconds to look at the walls crumbling down at another hit of the iron ball. Pointing to the building, a part of which still stood on its base, he continued, 'It was not a good design for this building. When a structure falls, each of its members should fall simultaneously, and it should fall on its foundation without swaying sideways. That is the ideal design. Limited State Design, we call it.'

Cawasji's eyes remained glued to the building. Ganeshan also kept looking at it, repeating foolishly what Cawasji said, 'Limited State Design.'

Cawasji turned to Ganeshan and smiled. Placing his hand on his shoulder, he said, 'If you can wait a few more minutes, we can go back together. We can have a game at my place. We are yet to play one that ends in stalemate.'

'Another day, Cawasji. I will head back now,' said Ganeshan.

Cawasji had already turned and started walking back without waiting for Ganeshan's reply. As if he knew that it was not yet time for that stalemate game.

Some more walls came down. Cawasji disappeared in the dust it raised.

Operators and supervisors waited for the dust to settle before going for the next hit.

Ganeshan felt a twinge inside as he stood looking at those houses. It was as if the air the walls and roofs had claimed to give shape to was now being returned to the atmosphere; once people had breathed it in, shared it with their loved ones, lent it their warmth. Sharing love and hope, desire and hate, passion, aversion…fathers and mothers, sisters and brothers, newlyweds…

FIFTY-FIVE

On his way back, the power went off again. This time it was the whole city. The city had no glow for the sky to reflect. It was like driving through a tunnel in complete darkness—only few metres ahead of the car visible, lit by headlights. He drove on complete intuition, with just the faith that a known landmark would not fail to appear somewhere. The many years he has spent in this city could not be in vain.

A candle was burning inside the house. But Naseema was not to be seen anywhere. When he called out to her, she replied from the outside. He had not noticed her standing there when we walked in.

'Darkness is that phenomenon which makes one look everywhere else except at what is in front of one,' Naseema quoted a saying, laughing.

'Naseema,' he placed his hand on her shoulder.

'Viewed from another angle,' she said, 'darkness, too, has its relevance. It makes us understand the value of light.'

'Certainly. And the value of many other things, too.'

'Like?'

'For example, of houses. Naseema, just try to remember the government colonies where we lived. The two-storey houses, painted yellow, with small open grounds between them. Wasn't there one on the northern end of the city?'

'Maybe. So?'

'That is being demolished. The whole colony. And that, too, is a pilot project.'

'Oh!'

'I saw it today. Cranes swinging huge iron balls and hitting them.'

'In darkness?'

'The darkness led me to the place. But what I mean…' Disappointed by Naseema's lack of interest, he left it at that, and asked, 'What were you saying about darkness and light?'

The discussion on darkness and light led them to Vasundhara. Naseema said that she would now be in the hospital for some time and that she was on drugs and was sedated most of the time.

'The treatment to mental illnesses these days is mostly by clinical methods with the help of medicines,' she said.

'The psychoanalytical methods are virtually out of practice. The deconstruction method is rejected at least in this case,' Ganeshan commented. 'A recent report that came in the papers where scientists working in the field were said to have concluded that children born to men above fifty years had increased chances of getting schizophrenia.'

Naseema reflected that Vasundhara was the most active member of Saathi. She liked her very much though they used to quarrel sometimes due to the differences in their personalities. Ganeshan didn't ask any more. Naseema, too, relapsed into silence.

The power problem appeared serious, there seemed to be little chance of early restoration. During dinner, which they ate in candlelight, Naseema wondered what all could happen in a city without light. When she retired for the night, Ganeshan knew that such worries would not affect her sleep. Sadhana and spirituality helped her win over worries. Ganeshan sat watching the candle burning, for some time and then in the candlelight read Aman's poem:

Walls are coming down.
Walls between heaven and hell,
The mighty and meek,
Man and woman, father and son,
The familiar and stranger
Are crumbling.
Everything seeps into everything,
Sometimes as a guest,
Or a chance caller,

As a violator, or as a friend,
As a relative, as an aquaintace,
As the breath that comes in and goes out,
The blood that flows within,
The lymph that circulates between tissues,
As the hernia of organs
That leave their own place and encroach.
Anyone can become anyone else.
Don't ask who is who,
Everybody is everybody.

For the first time, this question came to Ganeshan's mind: what was happening to Aman? He had been taking all that he had written, whether they were poems, songs or notes, as they were. But these days, he felt a little unsettled every time he read and pushed a page to the bottom of the pile. The new page sliding down and the next one revealing itself had together acquired a dynamic of their own. Like the shape-changing shadows that are alive, Aman was becoming a presence from absence, Ganeshan felt. A little while away, he had seen Cawasji emerging out of the dust cloud created by crumbling walls of the colony and with the same magical detachment, returning to it. The darkness that pulled Ganeshan, like a whirlpool, into that strange wilderness was still there. In the city, in his house and this room. But here, Aman, standing among collapsing walls, refused to disappear. He was there amidst the debris, reminding him that there were still membranes and tendons, invisible though they were, between the fragments of life…

The candle flame before Ganeshan flickered in the breeze coming in through the window, like a guest or chance-caller. It drew and redrew the constantly changing surrealistic pictures on the walls, with light and shadows. The flickering flame pushed down the molten wax. The sculptures made by molten wax were realistic compared to the pictures on the wall. But they, too, kept changing as more wax flowed down from the candle.

Ganeshan slid the poem of collapsing walls to the bottom of the pile. As he did so, he found that the poem on eternal city, the first one, had come very close to the top. Aman would soon bid goodbye. There were only two more pages for him to read. One below a blank page, and one more below yet another blank page. There was a strong temptation to read them right away, but he immediately controlled it. The rule was that only one at a time…What if the pages got over? He would return to the gates of the eternal city. And start from there again. Aman's papers were taking a life of their own. Aman was taking leave but to enter into perpetuity, not a void.

Zoya did not come to talk about Aman. She may not come now. Or she might appear again out of emptiness, one day, in the form of a greeting card bearing a painting conveying the experience of forlornness. After all, she was just a name given by Rishi. One name among the many before him, known and unknown. Names enter and exit. Like breathing in and out. Like the blood flowing inside. Like the lymph circulating between tissues…keeping us alive, life going…

FIFTY-SIX

Tarun Kumar's ability to manifest in unexpected places was nothing short of miraculous. While every such appearance of his did untie some knots, on the other end, it also wove in more loops, leaving the structure no less complex than before. That was the other amazing thing about him.

The inspector had not uttered Aman's name even once. Yet, like himelf, he too was discovering Aman more and more, Ganeshan felt. Not through his poems as Ganeshan did, but through myriad characters from Aman's life. Neither of them brought up the subject of Aman ever. But they knew that Aman was the one pulling the strings and bringing them together on the same track.

Ganeshan had called up Tarun Kumar for help with getting Seeta's body released. That did not work. But, while waiting in the hospital and police station for long hours, the inspector had given him an indication that the police had made some progress in Mansoor's kidnapping case. However, since the occasion was not appropriate, they didn't continue the conversation.

The occasion came up suddenly in the transport office. Ganeshan had gone to renew his driving license. He was standing in the queue with his forms, when Tarun Kumar appeared, as usual, out of the blue. Ganeshan was not surprised as such encounters were becoming the norm now.

The inspector snatched the forms from Ganeshan's hands. Ganeshan's pleas that he was not averse to standing in queues, that he rather enjoyed it had fell on deaf ears. The inspector said that he had things to discuss and that he needed Ganeshan to finish his work early. He went inside the office with the forms. He finished everything in minutes and came out. They went to a quiet corner and he immediately began his story.

'The breakthrough came last week. We had some information about the places where Mansoor used to camp. We kept an eye on them. Then, a sudden lead came last week, which sent us to a town some two hundred kilometres away. The local people told us about a hideout used by criminals. It was in the fields outside the town. Wading through vast yellow blooming mustard fields we reached a well and a pump house. There was an abandoned shed nearby which was locked from the outside.'

The inspector hailed a boy who was passing with a kettle of tea and cups. He needed a break perhaps to tell the rest of the story. Ganeshan was growing impatient.

'Mansoor's hideout was not at all in good condition,' he continued, sipping the tea. 'We tried to break the lock and the door itself gave away. Such weak doors protecting the strongroom of criminals. As soon as the door fell in, we were hit by a strong stench of rotting flesh. We pushed through falling birds' nests and hanging cobwebs into the room. There was a skeleton chained to the bars of the window. Yes, a chained skeleton! Worms had already picked the bones clean. A few tufts of hair, portions of jeans, shirt and shoes lay scattered. Worms had departed after finishing their work. The smell still remained.'

Ganeshan sought a bench to sit. His hand, holding the cup of tea, was shaking.

'Yes, sir,' the inspector said. 'When we shot Mansoor, we didn't know that along with a criminal, we had also killed a hostage-keeper. The hostage, too, died, but unlike the keeper, a slow death befell him.'

'The farmers in the field…they didn't hear any cry for help?'

The inspector shrugged. 'Human behaviour is sometimes inexplicable,' he said.

'And the second hostage?'

The inspector shrugged his shoulders. 'Where and in what condition, who can say?'

'Whose skeleton was it, inspector?'

'We have no proper description of the two people. The hair we found was black and the person was not too tall. The clothes and shoe were of local make. These details do not prove anything conclusively. They could fit foreigners, too. Then, of course, it could be of a third person even.'

'Yes, possible,' Ganeshan agreed.

As the inspector was taking leave, Ganeshan asked hesitantly, 'Inspector, what about Shukur?'

Tarun Kumar turned back and held Ganeshan's hands, whether in consolation or camaraderie Ganeshan didn't know. 'There are many things remaining, sir,' he said. 'Many things, many people…you know that what guides us policemen is a hope that all mysteries would one day be converted into evidence.'

He walked away without saying anything more.

FIFTY-SEVEN

Eight-feet long and six-feet wide rooms in a row. In every such room, a family of five or six members lived. The six feet front wall had a door, and the rest of the wall was unplastered brick. On the top of these rooms, most residents had added another room of the same dimensions. The ground floor rooms had concrete roofs, while the top ones, the unauthorised ones, had makeshift roofs of asbestos sheets, tin sheets, palm leaves or whatever other material they could lay their hands on. Walls of the top rooms were also of bricks, but mostly held together by mud mortar. The top rooms were generally rented out to other families. The access to top rooms was through a bamboo ladder placed in a slanting position from the ground. Each unit had a separate ladder. The ladder reached just up to the door of the top room, which was usually without a shutter. At the open doors sat women with their legs hanging down and with children in their lap. Children played on the ground in front of the shacks and on the ladders on which they climbed up and down. Food was cooking on chulhas made of old steel buckets. The rest of the ground was occupied by filth, pools of dirty water, flies and stray dogs. Children had defecated in different places. There were no latrines in the colony. People went out in the field for their needs. Water had to be carried in from the outside.

This was the picture of the colony of workers thrown out of employment that Koshi had mentioned. There were several units of such type, in many rows. Ganeshan's attention was so taken by the burning chulhas, pools of water, excreta and dogs, all of which had to be dodged while walking, that he forgot that he was searching for someone's house among them. Even if you searched, it was virtually impossible to locate a house, for there were no numbers anyway. Then it occurred to him that the slip Koshi had given also had no number on it! Koshi had only written down the directions to reach the place.

After going around the clusters for half an hour, Ganeshan was back where he started. No one there seemed to know a person called Koshi. If there was an addition to that name, his first or second name, Ganeshan didn't know it. Only one person among the ones he talked to showed any patience to listen to him. He seemed to know someone of the description Ganeshan gave but unfortunately had no knowledge of where he lived. And he added that this person had not been seen for some time. His best guess was that the man had left the colony.

Ganeshan gave up the search and returned to his car. Evening was approaching, and it was getting cold. He wore his pullover that he had left on the seat and started the car, abandoning Koshi to the endless labyrinths behind. It was futile to search for a person like Koshi, he told himself. Koshis can only be met by chance.

FIFTY-EIGHT

The first rains before winter fell. The day after the rain was warm, the daytime and nighttime temperature rising by a few degress. But from the next day, winter gained its vigour. The onset of winter in the city is like a celebration. That celebration was, however, stolen from Ganeshan and Naseema by Vasundhara's death.

It was certainly not unexpected, considering that her state of mind had been steadily declining these past weeks. She had relapsed into an amnesia and had become virtually cut off from others. Shamsher's death had breached the insulation her disease had built around her. She had recognised the picture of the man published in the papers and also seemed to be straining her failing eyes to read through the news. But then, suddenly, she pushed the paper away and dozed off. Her downward slide had started even earlier, and it was not clear if the incident dealt the final blow or not. She went from bad to worse, and finally took her own life. On the ride back from the hospital, she opened the door of the car and jumped out. The bus behind the car did pull its breaks, but it had hit her head before it could stop. Death was instantaneous.

Naseema was deeply affected. Her attachment with Vasundhara was stronger than Ganeshan had realised. Vasundhara was much younger than her, but she held her in high esteem. Naseema said that she used to take Vasundhara's side invariably whenever there was a clash of ideas in the meetings at Saathi. She didn't mention the numerous differences of opinion they have had.

On the first day, she put up a brave face. She didn't show any hurry to go to Vasundhara's house. But the next day, she went and remained there till the cremation was completed. The day after, she went to the ashram. And the day after.

Naseema appeared to be thoroughly exhausted when she returned from the ashram that evening. Ganeshan made coffee. They sat together at the table and drank it. Then she went and took a long bath. They had soup and bread for dinner, which Ganeshan had made ready in the meanwhile. As Ganeshan cleared the table after dinner, she took off her cardigan and sat down on the sofa, her legs fully stretched, head thrown back and eyes closed. She had reduced the volume of the TV to almost zero.

Sensing something out of place, Ganeshan went behind her and peered into her face. Her eyes were wet.

'Naseema?' he enquired. She shook her head.

Ganeshan touched her neck and forehead. She had no temperature, but he allowed his hands to remain and gently caressed her cheeks and neck.

After sometime she herself took his hands and placed them on her bosom, then gestured to him to come and sit by her side. When he did, she moved closer to him and lay her face on his chest and seemed to sag into him. He drew her to him and kissed her on the forehead and lips.

Months had passed since they had intimacy of the sort. They allowed it to develop, slowly but firmly.

It was Naseema who led Ganeshan to her room. She switched off the lights. Her bed, her smell, touch, all aroused him like days of their youth. Yet he felt that it was her desire that was leading him. It was her fire that set him burning. They didn't separate even after the fire burned down. She rested her head on his chest, but her hands explored him inch by inch as if discovering him anew.

'Naseema,' Ganeshan spoke first.

'If you don't mind, Ganeshan, call me Seema,' she requested softly.

'You are right. Every individual decides his or her identity by defining it, defining its limits,' he said laughingly. He brought his mouth close to her ears and said affectionately, 'Seema!'

She laughed noisily, like a little girl. Then she propped herself up on her elbow and lay there on her side looking into his eyes. He could see clearly the contours of her face in the light of street lamps coming through the window. He saw the emotions and sensuality of youth still reflecting on it.

'Human beings have an emotional life far richer and deeper than of any animal,' she said without taking her eyes off his. 'Do you know the reason, Ganeshan?'

'Tell me.'

She ran her fingers over his lips and then leaned over and kissed them. Then lowering her voice, she said, 'Only in human beings, male and female mate like this, face to face, looking into each other's eyes.'

'Oh Seema!'

He watched the passion slowly giving way to peace, with interest.

'Again, man has something that no other animal is gifted with: imagination,' she continued. 'Do you know the reason behind it, Ganeshan?'

'No,' Ganeshan shook his head like a schoolboy.

'Human beings are capable of controlling their emotions in a manner no other animal can. It is the same creative urge that gets expressed as physical desire, which motivates reproduction at one level, and imagination, which motivates art and literature. Human beings are uniquely capable of controlling the former and converting that creative urge into the latter. Animals cannot control their physical desires. If they don't go berserk, it is only because external factors sometimes prevent them. But man controls it by the internal strength of his self.'

'He limits it, I would say.'

'Doesn't the word Seema mean limit, Ganeshan?'

'One may say so.'

'Limit is defined distance. Distance is the point, Ganeshan…We have covered the distance we were required to travel. We have reached the seema.'

'What are you trying to say, Naseema?' Ganeshan turned to her, worry in his voice.

'Ganeshan, I am going to the ashram.'

'You are already going there, Na—sorry, Seema.'

'Not like that, I am joining the Mission.'

'Seema!'

'Swamiji has opened a branch of the Mission down south,' shedding whatever traces of emotion was left in her, and loosening her hands and body from him, Naseema explained the plan in a voice that indicated distance and detachment. 'It is Swamiji's wish that I should take responsibility of it. He has been telling me for some time. Today I gave my consent.'

'Oh!'

'Ganeshan, you shouldn't get upset. You won't feel lonely, tell me, promise me.' She placed her hand on his shoulder and looked down at him, 'Everything has a way and time, you know. I may come to the city in future, if the Mission sends me here…'

Ganeshan didn't say anything. He kept stroking her shoulder.

'At one stage, emotion ceases to be a spontaneous expression. It becomes one consciously produced, as imagination is,' Naseema continued in the same strain. 'We would be able to convert emotion into imagination and imagination into emotion. Every phase assumes the shape and role we give to it. Its size, spread, limits…If we define family by enlarging it to the size of the society…'

'Instead, we could also induct the world outside into the attributes we are familiar with, say, father, mother, sister, son… That may be easier.'

Naseema just kissed him on his chest once more and lay down next to him.

Soon he realised that she had fallen asleep. He pulled a blanket over her and went to the window and stood there, looking out.

Outside, the mist lay spread over the earth like a foamy blanket. It made the street lamps look like small dots. The buildings had disappeared behind it, but you could see faint outlines of lighted windows. They looked like orange-coloured rectangles floating in the air.

Ganeshan wondered why he brought up the analogy of shrinking the world outside into one's own circle. How was it different from her proposition? Or, perhaps it was different. Anyway, he was in no mood to pursue such thoughts. Only Naseema was on his mind; Naseema who was shedding her *grihasthashram* to embrace the *vanaprasthashram*.*

Some more orange squares switched off. Mist swallowed those houses, too. He remembered the dust from which Cawasji emerged and to which he disappeared, after warning, like a prophet, that more and more colonies were awaiting a death sentence. The dust which converted inhabited houses into just vacant space and remitted them back to the atmosphere.

*The Hindu texts mention four stages of life, or asramas. These are: Brahmacharya (education and celibacy), Grihastha (familial duties), Vanaprastha (spiritual exploration) and Sannyasa (renunciation)

FIFTY-NINE

Ganeshan was not sure what he wanted to tell him when he dialed Cawasji's number. That he didn't approve of the plan? Or perhaps he wanted to verify what he had witnessed that strange evening was indeed true. In any case, his call went unanswered. The answering machine said that his call had been recorded. After one hour, he called again and got the same message. He called in the evening, the morning next day, then noon. Every time the machine only responded.

As the calls remained unattended, his anxiety increased. Cawasji also had his office in the house. Even if he had gone out, someone else should have attended the call. Besides he had an attendant too at home.

The next day, he went over to Cawasji's house. He found the bungalow locked. The gate as well as the house. Dry leaves of trees had accumulated in the yard and in the porch, too. Dust had hardened with rain. It had been closed up for days altogether, it seemed. Ganeshan thought of enquiring at the nearby house. An old man opened the door.

'Cawasji?' the old man asked. 'You don't know? It has been a month since he died. It was in this very house that he was killed. Shot by someone. Two or three days had passed before it was noticed. The police have sealed the house. Better you don't go there.'

Ganeshan came and sat in the car. He couldn't take his eyes off the house of Cawasji. Instead of the picture of Cawasji at the demolition that had been haunting him for the last few days, now he could only think of him at the chess board with their glasses of whiskey on the table. Dust must have settled over that table and floor too, but his words about the games ending in stalemate still hung in the air.

Ganeshan drove from there to Rishi's place. Rishi confirmed the matter, 'Yes, the news had appeared in the papers sometime back. Architect found killed at his home, or something like that. It didn't occur to me that you had an architect friend.'

'Rishi, I had seen him only few days back,' Ganeshan said. 'We talked, not much of course. The occasion was not such. But he did propound one of his theories. That an ideal design is one where every member of the structure is of equal strength, so that when it falls, all members break simultaneously. Limited State Design or something he called it…there was a major power failure in the city recently, you remember? It was on that day.'

'I had gone for a drive in the evening,' Ganeshan continued. 'While returning, the lights went off, and I lost my way. I landed up in a colony, which appeared to be completely empty. The ghostly look apart, I found a strange sight there. In the floodlights powered by a generator, long cranes were demolishing the walls of the buildings, huge iron balls swung from the booms of the machines, smashing into perfectly functional buildings. They were dismantling the whole colony. It was in the midst of the dust that I saw him last. He told me they were starting a project to demoslish permanent structures and build temporary shelters in all colonies! He then invited me to his home for a game of chess. For a game ending in stalemate!'

'Which colony was that?' Rishi asked.

'I don't know the name. I accidentally ended up there after taking a wrong turn, you know. And it was dark.'

'Like the road you took was wrong, perhaps what you saw could also be wrong?' Rishi said that with a twinkle in his eyes.

Ganeshan laughed, albeit reluctantly.

'You said it was on the day of the power failure,' Rishi said. 'That date is easily found. As is the date on which Cawasji was killed.'

Ganeshan looked at him questioningly.

'Suppose the date of power breakdown was before the date of Cawasji's murder,' Rishi stopped.

'You talk like a police inspector, Rishi,' Ganeshan frowned. 'Anyway, such calculations do not seem relevant to me now. I look at it this way: three things happened. Cawasji has been killed. A colony was demolished. And I lost my way. All were wrong, and all happened together, like the Limited State Design!'

'Suppose one of them had not happened? For example, the demolition of the colony, then perhaps the others…'

'I also would like to believe so. That none of it happened, that the Limited State did not happen.'

Rishi placed his hand on Ganeshan's. 'What you said is right. This is not the time for calculations but for hoping.'

They were silent for some time.

Then Ganeshan asked, 'Do you remember, Rishi, what the dhaba manager said? That the children's band was disbanded? That they were scattered? Among the scattered was Imtyaz, Shukur's brother. He was one of the two boys who were kidnapped by the militants. The police have now discovered the body, rather the skeleton of Imtyaz, in an abandoned shed, chained to a window grille. The kidnapper happened to be the sustenance of the hostage. When the police killed the kidnapper, little did they know that a hostage was going to die with him. In fact, they didn't even know that their victim was a kidnapper. That band was like a broken colony. It collapsed, and every member fell apart. There are so many broken colonies in this world. And so many limited state designs…'

'A number of broken colonies. A number of disbanded bands. But Ganeshan, isn't it better to believe that no band would ever be totally disbanded? Music remains. Besides, who can say for sure that the skeleton they found was of Imtyaz?'

'What consolation is that? If not of Imtyaz, then another. If not of that band, then another.'

'In the same way, can we not hope that another Imtyaz would still be alive somewhere? Do you remember a habit you had that you have left behind? Of anchoring every event to Aman's disappearance, his return and finally to his death?'

After reaching home, Ganeshan placed a call to inspector Tarun Kumar. He had no direct knowledge of the case of Cawasji's death. Yet he made enquiries and called him back after some time. The investigation had not made any headway, he said. The reason was that it pointed towards Pappan's gang. Such cases reach nowhere. Police had been questioning people who were working with Cawasji because the murder had taken place in his residence. Tarun Kumar said that a driver who was with him had not been traced.

'Javed?' Ganeshan asked.

'I don't know the name,' the inspector said.

'Javed won't do that, inspector.'

'Do you know him?'

'I know of one Javed. He is a young fellow who sold his kidney for his sister's wedding. The recipient is searching for him, to write over his whole wealth by adopting him. But Javed does not want it, and he ran away from there.'

The inspector laughed. 'One Javed! How can you say if this Javed is that Javed? He could very well be another person. Besides, the police do not even suspect him.'

'You are right. He could be another person. In fact, I have not seen Javed. Why, I don't even know if his real name is Javed!'

Though he said he was not interested in calculations, Ganeshan took out the old newspapers that night. It didn't take much time for him to locate the paper he wanted. It was a Sunday paper. The report was in the city page. The noted architect of the city, Jahangir Cawasji was found killed in his residence. He looked up the projected time of death. It was almost the same time as he had met Cawasji at the demolition site.

SIXTY

The newspaper he had taken out from the old pile was still lying on his table, Ganeshan noticed two days later. The city page with the news of Cawasji's death was open. For a moment, he weighed whether to archive it. He decided against it. But he wanted to have another look at it before putting it back. Only a month old, yet it looked like an ancient document. Newspapers cross over to antiquity very fast. And then, like antiques, they become objects of curiosity.

He had not looked at the supplements, he realised. Being a Sunday issue, there were many. Long articles on new trends in films, bank scams and cookery. Below, an analysis on recurring floods and droughts, there was a half-page piece on the frauds in the arena of medicine. It should have been given under the article on bank scams. A good editor would have done so.

A small paragraph in it attracted Ganeshan's attention. 'Fake Transplants,' it was titled. The author claimed he had uncovered a new kind of scam, that some of the organ transplant surgeries were actually fake, which the abdomens of both the patient and the donor are cut open and stitched back up but no organs are tranplanted. Money would exchange hands, and it would be finally be declared that the patient's body rejected the transplanted organ.

That Javed need not be this Javed, Ganeshan told himself. That Javed need not be a fake donor. There are Javeds and Javeds in this world. So are there patients, organ donors, architects, Imtyazs, Vijays…

After a few days, Javed, who was Cawasji's driver, crossed paths with Ganeshan in the parking area of a public place. He was a parking attendant. He gave the coupon to Ganeshan and turned back. Ganeshan's attention was snagged by some eunuchs singing and dancing in front of a house on the opposite side of the road. Then his mind caught up, and he looked around. He was sure it was Javed. 'Oh Javed, one minute,' he called. 'Coming, sir,' the boy replied.

Javed didn't immediately return. He was driving a car out from the parking for its owner. Ganeshan got a few minutes to reflect. Then decided he did not want to meet Javed and without waiting for the man to return, walked away. The eunuchs were still dancing. He dismissed them also from his mind.

There would be so many Javeds in this world, he told himself again. So many patients, donors, architects, Imtyazs,

Vijays, boys forcibly castrated and made eunuchs, organs leaving their homes and encroaching other spaces as hernias or even transplants.

Ganeshan didn't tell inspector Tarun Kumar or Swami about his meeting Javed at the parking lot.

SIXTY-ONE

Once while going out, the older Aman had placed his hand gently on his shoulder, that was the most intimate occasion they had had, Ganeshan remembered. Apart from the day Aman had returned home after he went missing, when he had given him a hug, Ganeshan wondered if he had embraced him on any other occasion. There was no special reason for it on that particular day. In fact, he didn't even remember the day well. There was a small smile that hid behind his upper lip then, and a clearly visible shine in his eyes.

Each of the several pages he discovered in Aman's collection later, shook, attacked or rewrote the meaning and dimensions of the words: touch and distance. In a recent piece, he had written about the vanishing walls. In another, he wrote about his search for an old woman's son, who had come to the city from some faraway place, without knowing his name or description.

He spent three years with this boy who lived in his own space and time, without touching him, scared of touching him.

And when he finally came close to him through his writings, he was beyond touch. Ganeshan was unable to say if the poems and notes he left behind indicated a philosophy. If they did, his mind was not equipped with the faculties to assimilate it. He understood just one thing: the concepts he carried in his own mind about closeness and distance were loosening or changing.

Looking into his eyes, with her softly spoken words, Naseema, too, had tried to upend those concepts. Saying that the very same emotions, which draw man and woman together into the closest intimacy, when channelled in another direction, transform into imagination which flies to the limitless distances. Had Aman, in fact, begun teaching himself this process of converting emotions into imagination much earlier?

As he approached the last two pages of Aman's writings, certain things were becoming clear to Ganeshan. The tension in his mind regarding the ending of the pages was easing. The dynamics he himself had infused into them had rendered them endless. At the same time, as the pages were approaching a full circle, he felt that Aman was retreating from him gradually but painlessly, allowing the space vacated by him to be handed over to the realm of imagination.

It was evening. Naseema was yet to return home. The cold was gently permeating the air. Ganeshan went up to his son's room. He lit a candle for fear of the lights suddenly going off, which had become common since that major power failure.

In the next page, below a blank one, there was only one small note. He picked it up with the candle still in his other hand. He wondered why in his last phase, he took to prose:

These two kindhearted souls, whose son Aman I am not, have maintained a distance from me. Not for that reason, for they don't know that yet, but fearing that they may lose their son again. I, too, allowed the distance to remain, for fear of losing the distance itself! Have I not always been living in the distances, in the gaps and spaces? Percolating, seeping, melting into them? But that is really no solution to the problem. The problem remains, lives on…

Ganeshan sank into the chair. It shook the candle a little and a few drops of molten wax fell on his hand.

Below, he heard the click of Naseema turning the key into the lock. Then the sound of her steps, walking through the rooms, from one room to another, looking for him. The creaking of the kitchen door, the closing of the bathroom doors…

'Ganeshan,' finally she called, not seeing him anywhere.

'Yes, Seema,' Ganeshan replied from upstairs.

Hearing him addressing her as Seema, she chuckled.

'Oh, there you are,' she said. 'Dusting the room, eh? You could have done it during the day.'

'It is ok, it is not too dusty. I will be done in two minutes.'

'Okay, there is no hurry. Come down once you finish. '

'Yes.'

'Should I come and help?'

'No, no. I am nearly done.'

Ganeshan took only two minutes. Just as it took only two seconds for the hot wax burn to disappear.

So many things happened in those two minutes…

He had picked up that paper with a feeling of impending loss. That that connection with Aman was going to end. The first realisation was that that was not the end. It was like discovering there are more pages at the back for a good book you thought was about to end. It was like if, when walking towards a closed door, the door were to suddenly swing open. He did not know what was on the other side of the door. Did not know if the additional pages in the book had any writing on it. It did not seem relevant. It was like you got an extension to a deadline. The cyclical dynamics of the pages. Aman transforming from emotion to imagination. They were all devices he had created in fear of the void that was waiting in the future. He felt as if he got a new lease of life. The Amans, the children, they did not end there. They merely moved on. Like links in a chain, like sprinters in a relay race. That is not what he expected at all. The emotion that filled him, it was difficult to define it as happiness. But he knew that there was happiness somewhere. It may not be inside him. It may not be inside anyone. But it existed. Like the sun, even when one cannot see it. One knows that it will rise and bring warmth and life and hope. The dryness in Ganeshan's throat turned to moisture in his eyes. He picked up the bunch of papers and hugged them to his chest. He suddenly felt young.

SIXTY-TWO

Rishi had, the other day, reminded him of his old habit of anchoring every event to Aman's disappearance, return or death. He was not thinking of the oft-quoted axiom that time heals everything. He felt more like a state where all anchors were lifted. A better metaphor might even be a ground so fluid that no anchor can ever hold anymore. He was sitting on the veranda on an idle winter morning watching the blades of grass growing in the yard. One cannot actually see the grass growing. That is perhaps what the uncertainty principle of physics also says. By the time you focus your eyes on the blade of grass, it has already grown further and shifted to another position. The position and velocity of a moving object cannot be simultaneously observed at any given instant and hence the trajectory of the object remains undetermined. Not just the events of disappearance, return or death, here the uncertainty is at the root of the question itself. Whose disappearance, return or death?

Rishi himself was preparing to leave. His visa papers to go to Australia were ready. He refuted the view that anthropology was a backward-looking science. The attempt of any branch of science was to discover the essence of the phenomenon it is after and the laws governing that essence. So, one can say that all sciences are, in one way, inward looking. Truth is that the journey of science is un-anchored. Then, where is the inside or outside? He told Ganeshan that, by lifting his anchors, he, too, had joined the community of scientists. Rishi was surprised to learn that Ganeshan started off as a physicist.

Ganeshan said. 'I started from physics, the science of physical laws and have grown into biology, the science of exceptions!'

'That difference existed only until Schrödinger caught the cat and put it in the box,' Rishi said. 'Till he made it neither alive nor dead!'

'Wrong. Till he made it spirit and matter at the same time.'

Police officers no longer visited Rishi or Naseema to collect information about Seeta. Seeta and her death had very rapidly been reduced to a case number in the police file. Newspapers said that the case had already been solved, and the culprits had been put behind the bars. Media also revealed that the owner of the farmhouse, where Seeta was killed, was Kaku Supplier. Though the don was not found having a hand in the murder, the adverse propaganda would create inconvenience to the gang for some time. In turn, it might give a boost to their rival, Pappan's gang. Pappan had not yet been charged in the murder of Cawasji. His hold on Ashaniketan was likely to get tighter in the coming days. As Cawasji had retired from the scene, no more pages of the register of the home were forthcoming. No more barracks would fall. Those that fell would be reconstructed. And the missing pages of the register, too, would be repopulated, there will be more photographs of children.

One day, Ganeshan asked inspector Tarun Kumar if he could have the piece of paper with his name discovered among the Vijay's belongings. The inspector straightaway refused, almost rudely. 'That is evidence, property of the government. Why would you want it?' Ganeshan didn't really know why he needed it. He felt an affection towards it, that was all. Something inside him told him that it was valuable. Like the piece of paper extended to Aman by a mother at the bus stand was valuable to her. One may not qualify these as evidence. To be a piece of evidence was not the only way for a thing to become important.

Now Ganeshan was sure that inspector Tarun Kumar also knew that Aman was not Aman. That could even be one of the central points of his investigation. In any case, Ganeshan was not ready to change Aman's name, as he had done for Naseema.

Ganeshan felt that the question as to who was Aman was not key to his own investigations. Of course, the question of where his son was did occur to him. But he told himself that all were somewhere. If not here, somewhere. Like the branches of trees, like the trees of the forest, like the birds of the sky and like the stones lost, stolen, exchanged, retreived, renewed, or abandoned. There are gods of hope, despondency and imagination. Solving mysteries is energising for everyone like it is to policemen. But the entry of new characters must overshadow older ones in their files, too.

All mysteries should be solved, says reason. But unsolved mysteries sneak behind reason, mount on the horses of imagination and continue their journey, unlike the solved mysteries, which are readily forgotten.

Desouza asked about Aman's poems. How he came to know about them was a mystery to Ganeshan. He had thought that there was no space for poetry in the mind of the colonel who had lost a son and a daughter, one in action and the other under grievous circumstances. But when he asked, Ganeshan replied that Aman came like a poem but didn't go away like one. For poems don't go away, they remain forever.

That was when Desouza was recovering in the hospital after a stroke. When he returned home, he talked to Ganeshan about the school. Most of the staff in the school were volunteers, providing free service, he said. It was only proper for an organisation of that sort. Such an organisation cannot be a regular one after all. 'Paid employees, whatever be the organisation, at one stage or other, would ask for regularisation of service, confirmation etc.,' he said with a twinkle in his eyes. 'And confirmation of job, indirectly, would amount to acceptance of the permanency of the organisation, or say, permanency of the circumstances which made the organisation a necessity! We cannot have that!'

Then he went in and brought back a small notebook he used to carry with himself. Opening a page, he asked Ganeshan to read a poem written on it. It was written on top of the page that the lines were from 'Dover Beach' of Matthew Arnold and that they were copied from a book of a fellow officer.

'[…] the world, which seems
To lie before us like a land of dreams,
So various, so beautiful, so new,
Hath really neither joy, nor love, nor light,
Nor certitude, nor peace, nor help for pain;
And we are here as on a darkling plane
Swept with confused alarms of struggle and flight,
Where ignorant armies clash by night.'

There was a shadow on Desouza's face. After a few moments of silence, he said, 'Whether we like it or not, the circumstances that made the establishment of the school a necessity would continue permanently indeed.'

Desouza's wife had come when news of the stroke reached her. But she had gone back now.

Naseema, too, was getting ready to go. Pruning the collection she had spread on the bed, one by one, she brought down her luggage requirement to a medium-size suitcase she could carry herfself. Books and diaries were the major items. 'Clothes would be provided by the ashram,' she said. Even the name was to be provided by the ashram: Swamini Seemananda. In the evening, a van from the ashram would come to take her. Then onwards, she was of the ashram.

SIXTY-THREE

The last page Aman had left was short. Shortest of all. Just two sentences written in clear letters at the centre of the page:

There are limits to man's knowledge. But the fortunate thing is that he doesn't know where those limits lie.

Ganeshan stared at that page for a long time. At that page and at the shadows of the open gates of the eternal city that could be seen from below.

Then, breaking the sanctity and solitude of the notes, he stepped into them…picking up a pen, he wrote below the following lines:

Or by the time he discovers those limits, he would possibly have already crossed them.

GLOSSARY

Asha: Hope or wish

Baarat: A wedding procession

Balniketans: 'Bal' means child and 'niketan' means home; institutions for children, often providing shelter, education and care for orphans or underprivileged kids

Dada: Strongman

Grahastya ashram: One of the four stages of life in Hindu philosophy, referring to the householder stage, where one marries, raises a family and fulfils social and familial duties

Kabadiwallah: A scrap dealer

Kadhai: A deep, thick-walled cooking pot similar to a wok

Malkhana: A storehouse or repository at a police station for items seized during an investigation

Nariniketans: 'Nari' means woman and 'niketan' means home; institutions that provide support and refuge for women in distress

Razai: Quilt

Suprabhatam: Sanskrit for good morning. Here it refers to devotional hymns sung early in the morning in honour of a deity to start the day

Vibhuti: In Hindu tradition, sacred ash from religious rituals that is applied on the forehead as a mark of devotion

ACKNOWLEDGEMENTS

In one of her speeches, Mahasweta Devi mentioned an incident where a group of adivasis complain to her of another group stealing away their gods. The author is indebted to her for the phrase, *Stolen Gods* used in this book. The interpretations and ideas attached to the phrase in the narration are however the author's alone.

Isabel Fonseca, in her brilliant work investigating the life of the nomadic Romani people in post-communist Europe, *Bury Me Standing*, describes an instance of an old woman coming to her with a piece of faded paper and seeking her help to locate her son who had escaped to the city. The author acknowledges this small piece as an inspiration behind the incident described in chapter Forty-Two.